Dare to Trust

Dare to Trust

Portraits of Love
Book 4

Karen Rossi

A Karen Rossi Romance

Wisteria Publications

Wisteria Publications
507-4 Briar Hill Heights
New Tecumseth, ON
L9R 1Z7

Dare to Trust
ISBN: 978-1-988763-14-9
Copyright © 2018 by Kaarina Brooks

Published in Canada 2018

Layout and Cover Art by Taria van Weesenbeek

Please contact the author at brooks.kaarina@gmail.com for any questions or comments.

Dedication

Dedicated to my daughter, Katri, with love.

Other Books by Karen Rossi

"Portraits of Love" Series
    Dare to Dream
    Dare to Love
    Dare to Surrender

No Home for My Heart
Despite Everything
Beyond Forgiveness

Acknowledgements

I want to thank Taria van Weesenbeek who has given so generously of her time to bring this novel to life.

Chapter One

The lights of Lisbon receded slowly as the cruise ship headed toward the dark, open Atlantic. Angela Cordova had succeeded in securing herself a spot by the railing and now stood squeezed tight among the throng of passengers who had also come out to witness the departure. The pilot boat had just left the *Sea Princess* to make its own way on the Atlantic, until they reached the next harbour.

Sometime during the night the ship would head south, down the coast of the Iberian Peninsula on its way toward the Straight of Gibraltar, before proceeding on to the Mediterranean Sea. Angela hoped she wouldn't get seasick. The Mediterranean, she expected, would be small enough not to have the dreaded ocean swells that she now feared would spoil the Atlantic leg of the voyage. But that was nothing that a glass of beer wouldn't fix. Or so she'd been told. She wasn't much of a beer drinker, but if it kept her from experiencing motion sickness, she was all for it.

The crowd soon dispersed and returned inside to enjoy the evening's entertainment or to arrange their luggage in their cabins, but Angela remained on the deck and soon was standing there alone. She leaned her hands on the smooth wooden railing and gazed at the wake made by the ship, which then moved away as smaller and smaller waves. *Sea Princess* was not a huge ship, but was big enough that the top deck, on which Angela stood, was a fair distance from the surface of the sea.

She stood, deep in thought, leaning on the railing, and lay her cheek down on her hands, while below her the sea was getting darker. Soon she could only make out the white foam in the black water.

"Happy birthday, Angela!" she whispered and gave a huge sigh. Tomorrow night she would maybe celebrate with a glass of champagne, but tonight she was too tired from her travels. And besides, she wasn't too keen to remember that tomorrow she would be thirty-eight years old and traveling alone.

The few love-relationships she'd had over the years had all come to an abrupt end when she'd indicated she wasn't available for marriage—at least not without her mother coming along for the ride. Since her father had died fifteen years ago, Angela, an obedient daughter to the core, had been her mother's caretaker and companion until her brother had moved into the spacious Cordova mansion a year ago with his family. The love of his life, Marita, and their twin baby sons now delighted Mrs. Cordova, and Angela was no longer needed.

As the ship left the harbour, the wind picked up and tugged free a few wisps of dark hair from the tight bun at the nape of her neck. Angela tucked the stray strands behind her ear.

It wasn't like she had resented living at home with her mother. Not exactly. It was just that the years had passed by so quickly, and her mother had become more difficult and demanding as she aged. So the minute the twins were christened, Angela had moved into her own apartment, leaving Miguel and Marita in charge of the house and its mistress. Not having to take her mother's feelings into consideration at every turn should have been hugely liberating, but it had taken her a long time to reassure herself that she was really and totally free.

But after a year of living on her own and working in a little wool shop for pin money, she had decided this was not what she wanted to do for the rest of her life. Sure, it had been interesting, helping women with their knitting problems and showing them new designs—some of them her own—but the job hadn't exactly provided her with a fabulous income. Luckily she had a portion from father's inheritance to help ease the financial burden.

Being a companion to her mother, she hadn't pursued a university education, and had only taken a few interesting college courses over the years. And to pass the time she'd designed patterns and knit items for the wool shop customers, as well as having her knitwear on commission at the shop where she worked. They sold well, but there were only so many she could knit in a month using her own complicated designs. It was just a fun hobby, and she couldn't see it evolving into a money-making career.

But after a year, which she considered almost wasted, she wanted to come to a decision about what to do with her life. When she had seen the ad for this cruise in a travel magazine, she had impulsively—which was certainly not her usual *modus operandi*—reserved herself a berth, and had even paid extra for the single cabin. And because the cruise happened to take off right on her birthday, it seemed like it was meant to be. So here she was now, on a cruise ship, hoping the wide ocean would somehow open up her horizons and help her see some options for her future.

But she wouldn't think about that now. Like Scarlett O'Hara, she would "think about it tomorrow". Right now she had better go into the lounge and order herself that beer to stave off any possible queasiness when they had to face the ocean swells during the night.

Many of the passengers had gathered in the lounge, but there were still several empty tables around the edges of the room. Angela didn't know anyone at this point and, after the eight-hour flight to Lisbon from Toronto, she was too exhausted to strike up a conversation with anyone. So she settled down at a small table in a corner where she would have her beer and then retire to her cabin as soon as possible.

The waiter came up and she ordered her drink. Then, to make it clear she wanted privacy, she dug a pocket book out of her purse, removed the book mark and began to read.

During the night she woke to a gentle rocking motion that told her the ship was out on the Atlantic. It felt pleasant and she immediately fell back asleep, thankful the beer was working.

The morning the sun peeked through the large picture window of the Juliet balcony, waking her up. Angela turned in bed to look at the clear blue sky, which was all she was able to see from her prone position. The sun was shining, which couldn't help but make her feel up-beat. She jumped out of bed and hurried to open the sliding doors. The ship had docked at Portimao sometime during the night and for a while she stood there in her pajamas, watching the dock workers below her, as they engaged in their noisy bustle of activity.

A tremor of excitement coursed through her. She was so far from home. So far from anything familiar. It was a whole new world out there, just waiting for her to experience and explore on this first morning of her trip.

And it was the first day of her thirty-eighth year. That wasn't a big milestone, so there was no reason for a huge celebration, but today she would take the time to somehow mark the day. Thirty-eight! The number was no reason to celebrate. More like reason to rue the years gone by with nothing much to show for them. Her jubilant mood evaporated like the ocean spray and she pulled the curtains shut. Except—Angela reminded herself as she tied her long, black hair into a bun and headed for the shower—she was now embarking on a new phase of her life, so in a way, it *was* a milestone and even a reason to celebrate. As she soaped herself, she tried to think what she could do to make the birthday special. Despite the depressing number.

Sylvia's words rang in her ears.

"For God's sake, Angela, let down your hair and live a little," her best friend had said as they hugged goodbye at the airport in Toronto. "And remember, a cruise ship is like a little private world of its own. What you do on a cruise ship stays on the cruise ship. Nudge, nudge, wink, wink."

Sure thing, Sylvia. But Angela wasn't the kind of woman who just casually "let down her hair", even if no one would ever know about it afterwards. She wasn't on this cruise to engage in a furtive shipboard tryst. She was here to think about her future and to make some decisions as to what she should do for a living. Mother was no longer her prime consideration and she could now concentrate on herself. What a liberating thought! Funny it should have taken her almost a year to get used to the idea. Well, that was just the way she was. Not exactly Miss Impulsive. Not usually anyway.

Emerging from the shower, she slipped on a pair of khaki walking shorts, a light pink top and beige running shoes, ready for a day of exploring Portimao. Portimao! Even the name sounded exotic, so maybe something exciting would happen there. But—Angela shrugged pragmatically—more than likely not. It wasn't like her to get her hopes too high, but it would be interesting to see what that ancient city had to offer.

In the breakfast room most of the round tables were already filled as people were obviously keen to get on with the day. She found herself a seat and then ate her bacon, eggs and toast quickly, trying not to get too involved with her chatty, elderly tablemates. She definitely wanted something salty in her stomach, not knowing how long it would be till lunch.

The bus was already waiting on the dock and Angela was one of the first to get on. She chose a seat by the window, midway down the aisle. Passengers kept filing out of the ship and climbing onto the bus, chattering and laughing loudly. Soon almost every seat was taken.

"Excuse me, is anyone sitting here?"

The deep, masculine voice made Angela look up with a start. "No, no one is," she said.

The man's brown eyes twinkled with humour. "As I can plainly see," he quipped. "In that case, I hope you don't mind if I do."

"No, not at all." Instinctively Angela moved over slightly toward the window to make room for the man's broad shoulders.

As he settled into the seat, Angela looked at him surreptitiously. He was very pleasant-looking, perhaps around forty, with straight light brown hair that came over one brow.

"I saw you last night in the lounge," the man said, turning to her. "You were reading a book, and looked like you wanted privacy, so I didn't want to disturb you by coming over to introduce myself."

Too bad. It would have been much nicer to talk with him than read that silly book. In fact, it would have been good just to look at him. It was her own fault for making herself unapproachable.

"I'm Travis Jordan." He held out his hand in the small space between them.

"Pleased to meet you. I'm Angela Cordova." Angela shook his hand in the rather awkward position, and they both laughed.

"From . . .?"

"Toronto, Canada," Angela told him. "And you?"

"Also from Canada," the man replied. "But further west. Calgary."

To start a conversation, Angela wanted to ask why he was taking this cruise, since it seemed like he was also traveling alone, but she didn't want to have to reciprocate and tell her own reason for the voyage. Which was not that easy to talk about.

She hadn't really thought about what she would say if and when some traveling companion asked her. Of course it wasn't anyone's business, but she was sure someone would be curious enough to enquire at some point during the trip. "I'm trying to figure out what to do with the rest of my life," would sound very philosophical, and would elicit too many probing questions for which she had no answers.

The bus took off with a jerk and proceeded through Portimao, up a hill, and into the town of Alte. They only stopped there for a quick photo-op at the Church of Our Lady of the Assumption and continued into the town of Silves. Here everyone disembarked and Angela joined the group that started to walk up the hill toward the twelfth century Moorish Castle while the less adventurous passengers stayed behind to explore the area closer to the bus. She was happy to see that Travis had joined the walkers. He caught up with her at the front entrance to the castle, which was guarded by a huge statue of Sancho I of Portugal. Together they proceeded to walk along the ramparts.

"Quite the view," she remarked, stopping to gaze over the ancient town.

"Nothing like this in Canada," Travis remarked. "Which, of course, is the reason we're on this trip. Right?"

Was that a probing question or just a rhetorical observation? Angela decided it was the latter and simply said, "Right. Everyone wants to see something different from their usual surroundings."

They continued to circle around the ramparts, commenting on whatever either of them found interesting. At one point Travis stopped and pointed at a group of houses in the town below. "Look, aren't those storks up on the chimneys?"

"Oh, yes," Angela exclaimed, delighted. "One, two, three . . . four of them! I've never seen a stork before. Except in fairy tales."

It was a very fitting sight, since to her this cruise was

much like a fairy tale. But she was sure Travis would find such an observation silly, so she kept those thoughts to herself.

But he surprised her. "Fairy tales, eh?" Travis leaned his elbows back against the stone railing and faced her. "Kind of like this cruise. Right?"

"Oh? How is that?" Sylvia's words about letting her hair down echoed in her mind and she lowered her face to hide the blush that rose onto her cheeks. She was sure that was *not* what Travis was thinking about.

"I've found that things that happen on a cruise aren't real. What I mean is, they're real just for the week or two, and after the cruise is over, they evaporate, kind of like Brigadoon. People go their own ways, never to meet again."

So he was kind of circling around Sylvia's words. "You think so? That sounds rather sad," Angela said. "Never to meet again."

"I know so. I've seen it happen on other trips I've been on. You know, conferences and such. You meet interesting people and although you might really hit it off with someone, you never keep in touch afterward beyond the exchange of a few pictures. Maybe a Christmas card if things really clicked. But somehow it all just ends when the trip is over, or shortly after."

Angela looked out over the valley. "That sounds so unfortunate. I mean, what if you really get along well with someone?"

"Yes, even then. That's just the way it always seems to happen. Relationships just evaporate after a while. Haven't you found that to be the case?"

"I've never actually been on a cruise like this before," Angela confessed, feeling slightly embarrassed. Or to a conference, either, she wanted to add, or on any longer group trip. But she really didn't care to expose her lack of travel experience because it wasn't his business to know. Thinking back to the chatter at the breakfast table, it had sounded like most of those people were seasoned travelers like he, and she didn't want to come across as a blue-eyed babe. "But my friend told me that a cruise ship is like a little world of its own. Is that true? Kind of like your Brigadoon?"

Travis grinned and she was delighted to see how the smile created tiny wrinkles at the corners of his eyes. "Your friend is right on the button, there. It's so easy to become intimate with your fellow passengers. Sometimes you exchange secrets you'd never normally tell to anyone after such a short acquaintance."

"Really?" That sounded much too intimate for her. Her sense of privacy would never allow that.

"Yes. I think it's exactly because you don't expect to ever see this person again that makes you open up to him or her about your life," Travis explained.

"I think in today's society there is already way too

much disregard for one's personal privacy," Angela exclaimed. "I would not want to do such a thing."

Travis shrugged. "Yes, but it happens."

They continued to stroll along the ramparts to view the town from the other side.

"So this is your first cruise then, eh?" Travis asked casually. It didn't sound like he was probing, but merely conversing.

"Yes, it is. And if I don't hit it off with anyone, then there will be no problem if we lose contact. Right?

"That's true," he agreed. "But more than likely you'll meet at least one person on this trip with whom you will hit it off. That generally happens."

Angela turned and began to negotiate her way down the steep, uneven stone steps. "Well, it really doesn't matter, does it? As you say, after exchanging a few photos the contact will be over, so . . ." She shrugged, and tried to say it in as carefree a tone as possible, hoping he would understand that it wasn't something she considered important. However, in her mind she somehow didn't like to think of this outcome.

Soon they were back at the grand castle entrance and joined the others from their bus group who had stayed behind.

"Hey, you should at least have a couple of photos to exchange with that someone with whom you aren't planning to hit it off," Travis said and pointed his camera at her. "That didn't come out quite the way I intended, but you understand, I'm sure."

Angela laughed. "Yes, I get it, even though you said it in a very convoluted way."

"I'll send you a shot of you beside this monstrosity the guide book calls 'the imposing statue of Sancho the First of Portugal'. Okay?" Travis said and pointed his camera at Angela, who smiled and struck a deliberate pose.

"So then does that make you the person I am supposed to hit it off with? she asked.

"Yes. Definitely." Travis pocketed his camera and offered her his arm as they got ready to board the bus. "Shall we begin right now?"

"I'm not sure, but I do want to have a few pictures of me, and not just of the group or the scenery," Angela smiled, but didn't take his proffered arm. "I want to prove to my friends that I was actually here."

As the bus headed back to the docks to drop them off at the ship for lunch, Travis again sat beside her. At first Angela thought he did it because he just wanted to sit beside her, but then she noticed that everyone occupied the same seats as before. She made a mental note of that, so she wouldn't mess up the seating plan on future shore excursions.

"Would you have any objections if this Westerner joined you for lunch?" Travis asked as they walked up the gangplank.

Angela took the disinfectant towel the steward handed her at the door and wiped her hands. "No objection. This Southern Ontarian would be very happy if he did."

"Formal or informal?" he asked.

She discarded the towel into a bin. "Definitely the most informal possible."

Travis laughed. "A greasy sandwich on a deck chair with a bottle of beer?"

Angela grimaced. "A bit more formal, then."

After they each had picked out their lunches from the menu in the ship's café, they found a small table by a window and sat down.

He took a bite of his burger. "So, what are you doing this afternoon?"

"There's a group going back to Portimao, but I think I'll just sit in the lounge and read," Angela said, and then added, "I may even have an early happy hour." She wanted to let him know he was under no obligation to spend his afternoon with her. As far as she was concerned, he was free to go his own way, with whomever he wished.

"I was hoping you'd come to Portimao and explore the town with me," Travis said, causing a slight blip inside her breast. It was nice to know he wanted her company, but after their conversation on the ramparts, she was on her guard against possibly starting a—whatever they had been talking about this morning. They hadn't actually given it a name, only mentioned "hitting it off" with someone. So, what would that be called? A friendship? A shipboard romance? She assumed "hitting it off" could run the gamut from one to the other. But whatever it was, she didn't want to start one.

Sorry Sylvia. She knew she would be going totally against her friend's advice.

Spending an afternoon by herself reading was something Angela was quite used to doing when she had lived with her mother, and now made it easy for her to accept the presence of the few elderly passengers. But after a couple of hours trying to concentrate on her book, she began to wish she'd opted to go on shore with the group instead. No, it had nothing to do with Travis. It just was a shame to sit in the near-empty lounge, listening to the hum of quiet conversation. That, and piano player half-heartedly plunk out some familiar melodies was lulling her to sleep.

She looked around the lounge and saw she was the only younger person in the room. The realization now struck her in the face. What was she doing here? Most of these people had probably passed on the outing because they had problems moving around. She was definitely in the wrong company. It was her birthday, for goodness sake! She should have been doing something exciting instead of sitting here reading. Like exploring the ancient town of Portimao. In the company of Travis.

Ho-hum. She closed the book on the bookmark and looked around at her elderly companions in the lounge. But perhaps in some of the cabins there were young lovers spending the afternoon doing what young lovers did best. Now what on earth made her think of such a thing? Of course! It was the romance novel she had been reading, where the hero and heroine engaged in fairly hot love-making at regular intervals.

Angela tucked the book into her purse, got up and went out for a stroll on the deck. When was the group from Portimao due to arrive, for goodness sake? Back and forth she paced, climbing from time to time to an upper level deck or descending to a lower one for a change. This was it! She would never stay behind again, no matter what the destination.

After what seemed like hours, the bus brought the explorers back and Angela listened enviously as they chattered on about what they had seen. Most comments she heard were positive, but of course there always had to be someone who wasn't satisfied with the excursion.

"So many of the stores were closed," one woman

complained. "You'd think they would have their siestas later in the day and kept the stores open for the tourists."

Angela was just heading for the lounge to order a pre-dinner drink, when she heard her name being called. She turned around and was pleased to see Travis hurrying to catch up with her.

"So what did you do all afternoon?" he asked, falling into step beside her.

"Just read, like I said I would," she answered. "But I've decided I'm not going to miss any more shore excursions."

"Bored?" he asked and grinned knowingly. A cute dimple appeared on his left cheek.

Angela grimaced. "To say the least. I didn't pay all the money for this trip to sit by myself all day."

Travis nodded. "Serves you right for not coming to keep me company. I missed your views and comments. But would you join me for a glass of your favourite brew after I get cleaned up? Or have you already had your happy hour, like you said you might?"

"No I haven't. And I'd be glad to join you." More than glad! She was delighted. Since he was the one making the invitation, it indicated he wanted to be with her. She could now relax and not worry that he was stuck with her while rather being with someone else.

In the dining room they sat at a round table with several other passengers. Everyone seemed to think they were a couple, and Angela didn't feel like starting a lengthy conversation in order to set the record straight. She decided to let Travis do the explaining but for some reason he, also, let the matter lie.

Their table companions—all six of them—were Americans and obviously had traveled far and wide. They regaled the group with stories of amusing vignettes from their trips, making Angela feel like a total outsider. Even Travis recounted a couple of humorous anecdotes from his travels, but she had absolutely nothing to add to the conversation. No one would find her story of a weekend spent at a friend's cottage very exciting, even if tipping the canoe over had been kind of funny. So she decided to keep her mouth shut unless someone asked her a direct question.

Which came soon enough.

"Don't you agree there's no other sea as blue as the Aegean?" The woman's question was directed at Angela.

"I'm afraid I have never had the pleasure of seeing it," she replied.

"Oh, really? Then you'll get a lovely surprise when you do see it," the lady assured her.

Angela smiled. "That's very nice to hear." *If* she ever got to experience that pleasure. But of course then the

blueness of the sea wouldn't come as a 'lovely surprise'.

"And you'll find the Greek Islands are *so* full of history," an elderly gentleman told her, as though he assumed cruising on the Aegean was now at the top of
Angela's bucket list.

Angela nodded, smiling. "I'm sure they are." She
couldn't decide if these travelers were trying to impress
each other with their vast knowledge of the world, or
were they just telling of their experiences to an appreciative audience. She decided it didn't matter what
their reasons were. After all, why bother to travel if you
couldn't share your adventures with others? Would
she be like that after she got home from this cruise?
"Sylvia, you won't believe the size of that statue of Sancho the First of Portugal!" She hoped she wouldn't.

After dinner she and Travis headed to the lounge
where the music was already playing. The pianist did-
n't seem to have much luck wheedling the over-stuffed
passengers to get up and dance. But the four-course
dinner obviously hadn't had a soporific effect on
Travis, for as soon as they found a table, he turned to
her.

"Please dance with me," he said.

"Dance?" Angela knew she sounded gob-smacked,
as though he'd suggested they do a few synchronized
somersaults on the floor. Though she'd taken ballroom

dancing a few years ago just for something to do, it hadn't been much fun without a partner of her own so she'd quit after only a few classes.

"I . . ." she began. "I have—"

"Listen!" Travis exclaimed, his brown eyes sparkling. "He's playing *The Piano Man*! We *have* to dance this one!" Without waiting for her to respond he took her hand and pulled her toward the empty dance floor. It would have been silly to struggle in front of everybody so Angela came along. And the next minute she was glad she'd agreed.

With a wide, boyish grin Travis took off, leading her in the fast waltz, twirling her around the floor at a dizzying speed. Only a handful of couples joined them, so they had almost the whole floor to themselves. He moved so quickly that Angela felt she was flying through the air in circles. Her feet moved nimbly, barely touching the ground—one, two, three; one, two, three.

She laughed with exhilaration and felt like a southern belle with a wide hoop-skirt, being whirled around the floor by her beau. This was fun. No, this was fantastic! Never before had she danced with anyone who had such a masterful hold on her. At intervals he changed direction, carrying her with him. There was never any fear that she might fly off or stumble, as round and around they spun like a single spinning top, his strong arm supporting her back.

When it was over, he led her back to their table. She was panting, but he merely took one deep breath and let it out in a satisfied sigh.

"That was great!" He pulled out the chair for her. "Thank you."

"It was totally my pleasure." Angela exhaled. "In fact, it was so good that I will consider it my birthday present. Thank you."

Travis frowned. "Birthday?" He pulled out a chair for himself and sat facing her.

"Yes. But it's not a big special one, so I didn't want to advertise it. However, it would be a shame to let it go by with no one knowing but me. In fact, I was planning to order some champagne to celebrate. I would love it if you helped me drink it."

"Gladly!" Travis signaled the waiter, who came right over. "It's the lady's birthday," he said. "Could you please bring us a bottle of your finest champagne. And I think she should be able to request her favourite piece of music. Right?"

"Happy birthday," the waiter said with a slight bow to Angela. "What would you like me to ask the pianist to play?"

Angela thought for a minute. "I'm sure he knows *The Unchained Melody*."

A slow piece had already started. Travis rose and

made a courtly bow. "While we wait for the champagne, may I have this dance?"

He held her close, and as they swayed to the slow beat she slipped her hand around the back of his neck. Why not? It seemed the right thing to do under the circumstances. Obviously encouraged by her move, Travis tightened his hold on her and she could feel the whole length of his lean body as it moved smoothly against hers. She couldn't deny that this was the most thrilling thing she had ever experienced.

When the piece was over they returned to their table and at that point the piano player made his announcement. "The next dance is for a lovely lady who is celebrating her birthday today. I'd like to ask her and her beau to start the dancing."

As soon as he began to play *The Unchained Melody* Travis rose and held out his hand to her.

"Yes," she said almost dreamily, in response to his unspoken question and gave him her hand. Yes, she wanted to dance with him. Yes, she wanted to have his arm around her. And yes, she wanted to feel again his body move against hers.

Travis guided her onto the floor, his hand on the small of her back. The pace was dreamy and he held her close as they slowly swayed, the only couple on the floor. Somehow his moves seemed even more sultry than before and she really should have tried to prevent their bodies from touching so intimately. She didn't. Hot fires coursed through her. The dance was so sensual she absolutely did not want to move away. She couldn't.

Other couples were now joining them on the floor. As they passed, a few of them called out birthday greetings to her, to which Angela responded with a smile and a nod. She almost wished they would ignore her, because the greetings were an interruption that prevented her from concentrating on the erotic feelings Travis roused in her. He bent his head and laid his cheek on her hair and she felt his breath against her face. Hot sensations tingled down through her body.

"You dance beautifully," he whispered.

Angela knew she was no Ginger Rogers, but at this point she was ready to believe whatever he said. Even if she knew he was spewing nonsense, it sounded so lovely and so right for this magical night.

At their table an unopened bottle of champagne in an ice bucket was waiting for them, along with two flutes. Two slices of delicious-looking cake also had appeared and one had a small candle stuck in it.

The waiter returned and lit the candle with a flourish.

"Don't forget to make a wish," Travis reminded her. Unnecessarily.

What should she wish for? Something practical or

something totally frivolous? But even though she knew this was all silly nonsense, yet she couldn't help putting some thought into the wish before blowing out the little candle.

I wish that on this voyage I will find the answer to my future.

Pouff! The candle was out and her wish rose toward the ceiling in a curling wisp of smoke.

"There," Angela cried. "Now I just have to wait for it to come true."

"Any wish made on a cruise ship will automatically come true," Travis pronounced solemnly. "It's decreed in the *Law Book of the Seven Seas*." His eyes twinkled.

"I didn't know there was such a book," Angela said with a smile.

"There probably isn't," he replied. "But there should be. The Seven Seas need some laws to keep them functioning properly."

With much ado, the waiter popped the cork of the champagne bottle and poured out the sparkling, bubbly liquid into the flutes. "Many happy returns," he said and withdrew.

Travis raised his glass and smiled. "Happy birthday, Angela," he said. The dimple on his left cheek added charm to the words.

They touched glasses and Angela took a gulp of her champagne. "I know you're supposed to sip it," she apologized. "But I really do like champagne and I don't want to let this bottle go to waste. We have a huge job ahead, because I want us to finish it."

The deep sound of Travis's laughter made something very pleasurable stir inside her.

"I agree totally," he said. "And we want to finish this, too." He took a big forkful of his cake. "Yummy," he declared and wiped the creamy icing off the side of his mouth with his fingers.

Angela pulled out the candle, licked the end, and helped herself to a forkful of the cake. "You're right. This *is* delicious."

They washing the cake down with plenty of champagne, but still Angela eyed the bottle suspiciously. "Do you think that is the normal size? To me it looks bigger."

"It's the normal size," Travis reassured her. "And don't worry, we'll have no trouble finishing it tonight."

Angela was already feeling the effects of the alcohol in her head. "At this rate, you'll have to carry me to my cabin," she said with a giggle which surprised her and caught her off guard. She was not a giggly kind of person. In fact, she hardly ever giggled.

"I'd be more than happy to oblige," Travis said, saluting her. "But first, maybe you'd like to take a walk on the deck? I think there's even a full moon out there celebrating your birthday."

"As long as I can exit without making a fool of myself," Angela said, getting up.

With his arm around her waist, they walked without a mishap toward one of the doors that led outside, and then continued along the deck until they found a spot by the lifeboats where the lights barely reached. No one else was around.

Angela looked up at the dark sky. "There is no moon at all," she said. "Where did you get the notion it might be full?"

Travis grinned. "It was just a ploy to get you to come out," he said, and then added jubilantly, "It worked."

"That is not why I came," she protested.

"So why did you?" The question was asked in a teasing tone and she decided to play along.

"Oh, I came out to see what else this magical, Brigadoon, fairy tale, birthday night had in store for me," she said, but she was only half-joking. Actually it was the truth. She had wanted to come out to see if this magical night had even more exciting things to offer.

"Why don't we wait and see if something happens," Travis said, no longer sounding like he was teasing.

Chapter Two

Side by side they leaned against the railing and listened to the whooshing of the wake against the hull. With no moon in the sky, the dark water was only lit by the lights from the ship. The beams were broken by the moving water so that the crests of the small waves glittered like diamonds. The ship had left Portimao while they were having dinner and was now heading toward Seville.

Angela's hand was resting on the railing and Travis placed his on it. Funny how that slight gesture had an arousing effect on her whole body. Her wayward body. But it wasn't entirely her fault, she argued with herself. It was the Brigadoon, the fairy tale, and the birthday magic surrounding them. And most of all—she had to admit—it was the champagne.

Travis gave her hand a slight squeeze. "Your hand is cold. Are you getting chilly out here in the night wind?"

Chilly? *En the contraria!* If he only knew. "Yes, let's

go in," she said.

"But before we do—" Travis leaned over and planted a soft kiss on her lips. "Happy birthday, Angela," he whispered.

Angela resisted the urge to thank him. He had barely touched her lips, but the soft kiss had the effect of changing the night into something magical. Just as she had hoped.

They settled down at their table again and continued their efforts to finish the champagne. After a while Travis said, "I want to show you something. Will you wait while I get it?"

"Of course." What did he want to show her? She couldn't guess.

He returned after a few minutes, carrying a large pad of paper, which he placed in front of her. "I drew this last night while I was watching you read your book."

Angela stared in surprise. There was no mistaking that the pencil sketch was of her.

"I hope you don't mind, but I found you so attractive with your proud head and graceful neck, and your hair gathered up in that bun. A beautiful Spanish señorita."

"Third generation," Angela corrected him. "But this is very good. You are an artist."

Travis closed the pad and laid it aside. "Yes, you're right. I went to college to become an artist. But landscape designing is my specialty. Gardens and courtyards and such. Which is why I'm on this voyage. I was in Italy, designing the gardens and surroundings for a new building, and decided to combine business with pleasure."

"My brother is also an artist," she told him, to stave off the question of why was *she* on this voyage.

"Is he? In Toronto?"

"Yes, he has a graphic design business with two other men. They met in Art College and—would you believe it?—they're all called Michael. I think that's what drew them together in the first place. Now they're not only business partners, but also best friends."

"What's the business called?" Travis asked. "I may have heard of it."

Angela took a sip of her champagne. "It's Triple M Graphic Art and Design. Of course the Triple M stands for Michael, Miguel and Mika."

"Can't say I'm familiar with it," he said. "But that's understandable since I'm in a different line of art."

"True. They also are creative artists and they all paint. Plus they take turns giving art lessons. My brother has a wife, Marita, whom he adores. And they have the sweetest little twin boys, André and Alexander. Michael is married to a young lady, Shaylee, who is also an artist. They've just had a baby girl whose name is Aurora. Mika is in Finland, teaching Canadian art history at the University of Helsinki. He found him-self a Finnish lady with three kids and is staying there for the time being. He is of Finnish descent but doesn't speak the language. Kind of like my relationship with Spain and Spanish."

Angela knew she was chattering, sharing way more than Travis had asked for about her brother and his partners. Perhaps this was what he meant when he told her that people on cruise ships tended to open up about themselves. At the same time, at the back of her mind, was the thought about how she would respond when he asked the inevitable question.

And then he did.

"So why did you decide to come on this cruise?"

"It's something I've always wanted to do," she said. "Visit 'the land of my ancestors'." She laughed and put air quotes around the well-worn cliché. It was true, be-cause a Mediterranean voyage and a visit to Spain had been on her bucket list for years. Of course that wasn't the real reason she was here, but there was no need to go into the details of her personal life. That reason should suffice. However, it did occur to her that nei-ther of them had brought up the question of why they were each traveling alone.

"Would you like to dance this number?" Travis asked. "It sounds like fun. Some kind of cha-cha, I think. I'm not good at identifying these Latin rhythms, but we could see if we can catch on."

Although it would have been wonderful to be in his arms again, Angela didn't think dancing a fast number was a wise move. The champagne bottle was empty and she was still standing on her own two feet—though only just. And so far she hadn't said or done anything terribly out of character. But getting up to dance a fast number definitely didn't seem like a wise move.

"Maybe we'll wait for a slow one," she said. Besides, this piece wasn't the kind where she could dance close to him and feel those sweet sensations inside her. Those dances were the best. Yes sir, they sure were. The best.

When a slow number started and Travis asked her to dance, she got up cautiously and then leaned heavily into him as they danced. She definitely did not feel like she was light and airy on her feet.

"I dance like an old cow," she grumbled, causing Travis to burst out laughing.

"No, you do not," he comforted her. "But I don't think this would be a good time to dance a fast waltz," he added with a chuckle.

"I don't think champagne is conducive to great dancing," Angela concluded. She didn't like the heavy feeling in all her limbs. "It is probably better for carrying on a conversha-shon." She giggled at her pronunciation but then said soberly, "I never gig-gle."

"A giggle now and then is perfectly okay," Travis said.

After the dance ended he led her back to the table where Angela mused about the evening. Despite the effects of the champagne and the birthday magic, in-cluding his kiss, she was not ready to let her hair down. In fact, in her slightly tipsy state she felt she should be careful and watch what she said and did.

So, sorry, Sylvia, not tonight.

Angela stretched, slid out of bed, and waltzed off to open the sliding doors. She was relieved she didn't feel the effects of the champagne at all. It was another beautiful day. The wake swooshed far below her bal-cony window and the sunny, sparkling ocean stretched out as far as she could see. There was no land in sight.

In the shower she soaped herself along the slender curves of her body and recalled how Travis's hands had felt, holding her as they danced. And they had kept on dancing—at times quite sensuously—till the tired pianist had called it a night by firmly closing the lid of the piano. Laughing like a couple of kids they had left the lounge, his arm firmly around her waist.

She came out of the shower, wrapped herself in one

of the luxurious, pure white towels and then stood by the open sliding doors, letting the ocean breeze waft her long hair around her head. She felt free and liberated like the ocean spray and took a few dance steps around the cabin. This buoyant, happy mood had to be totally the result of last night's birthday magic and dancing with Travis. And perhaps even the after-effects of all the champagne.

But now it was day and Brigadoons had a tendency to disappear in bright sunlight. Angela sighed. Sad but true. She must not expect Travis to be there for her today, ready to carry on like last night. After all, there were many other women on board whom he might want to get to know. Angela was not about to command his attentions for the duration of the trip for herself. Not even on the basis of last night. Last night was last night and today was today. It had been wonderful, but she had to be realistic. They were both free to meet other people and perhaps each of them would "hit it off", as Travis had said, with someone before the voyage was over. Who knew?

Why did she have to tell herself all this in rather severe tones? Perhaps because she was steeling herself for their inevitable meeting at breakfast and wanted to make sure she would strike a casual tone, like they were just shipmates who had shared a pleasant evening celebrating her birthday. It was Seville today and Seville would be an interesting experience. Even without Travis.

In the breakfast room most of the round tables were already filled and people were obviously keen to get on with the adventures that awaited them. At the far end of the room, Angela saw Travis in animated conversation, sitting next to a beautiful woman. There were still a couple of empty chairs at the table—one beside him, in fact—but Angela pretended not to notice, and seated herself at the other side of the room. Just because they'd danced a few dances the previous evening she was definitely not going to assume he was waiting for her to join him.

After breakfast Angela filed out of the ship with the other passengers, heading for the bus that would take them sight-seeing. Like yesterday, she found herself a seat in the bus and like yesterday Travis appeared and asked her if he could sit beside her. Something skipped inside her in a most delightful way. He wanted to experience Seville with her!

"You didn't come and join me for breakfast," he said with a slight rebuke in his voice as the bus took off. "I kept the chair beside me empty for you. Some of the people at the table who'd seen us together wondered why my travel companion didn't come. They even theorized that you were seasick and didn't want to have breakfast. I, of course, figured you were nursing a huge hangover."

"Oh, good grief, no!" Angela cried, laughing. "I hope you didn't tell them that! I just found a table that was almost empty and—"

"I didn't see you come in, or I would have waved madly to attract your attention."

Angela felt a slight stab of guilt for having deliberately ignored him. But, after all, he'd been having a lively conversation with that young lady beside him. She glanced around the bus and noticed the woman nearby, sitting beside a man, rebuking him for having forgotten the camera on the ship. Obviously a husband and wife team.

Angela grimaced. Served her right for jumping to conclusions. She could have enjoyed Travis's company at breakfast if not for her . . . jealousy? Surely not! She had simply tried to be accommodating and not assume he was hers alone.

The bus left the dock area and headed for the Plaza de España on the edge of Maria Louisa Park. Angela was relieved the subject of breakfast seating was forgotten as they pointed out interesting sights along the way to each other.

"Have you been to Spain before to explore your family's roots?" Travis asked.

"No, I never have. It was my grandfather who came to Canada originally, so it's been many, many decades since there's been contact with any relatives in Spain. You see, my grandfather didn't know how to write, and since letters were the only way to keep in touch in those days he soon lost contact." She shrugged. "That's how it was, way back then."

Travis nodded. "Yes, I can see that. It's a totally different story with today's immigrants. There are so many ways to have immediate connection to every corner of the world."

In the María Luisa Park they strolled past the beautiful tiled alcoves, each one uniquely decorated to show the glories of the province it represented.

"I can't believe how many provinces there are in a country this size," Angela remarked. "Some of our provinces in Canada are as big as Spain itself."

"You're right. But what really grabs me is the way this park simply abounds with wonderful gardens and boulevards," Travis enthused. "They're everywhere. I hope we have time to explore at least some of the gorgeous fountains and the botanical wonders. But I think I'll have to return here on my own to really take it all in."

Angela flipped through her itinerary. "Santa Cruz is supposed to have old Moorish architecture. I'm looking forward to seeing that."

Later, as they slowly wandered with their group along the extremely narrow, cobblestoned streets of

Santa Cruz, it was impossible to keep too far apart. This suited Angela very well for she had already decided she might as well enjoy each moment with Travis. He was an agreeable, enthusiastic travel companion and she couldn't have wished for anyone who was more fun to be with.

At one point Angela almost tripped on one of the many uneven paving stones and Travis quickly caught her arm.

"I'm surprised there aren't a ton of tourists with twisted ankles in Santa Cruz," he said. "These stones sticking up are just waiting to catch unwary people and give them a tumble." Then, instead of letting her go, he kept her arm tucked under his. "I'm going to keep you safe, you clumsy young lady."

Angela laughed. "Until you trip yourself."

Travis flexed his biceps. "Never! I'm as solid as the Rock of Gibraltar."

"Which we'll visit tomorrow, as a matter of fact. I can't wait to see the famous monkeys."

They remained close to each other throughout the morning, even while visiting the home of Bartholomé Murillo, a painter from the 17th century.

"Slightly different style from my brother's," Angela commented. "Miguel likes to paint curvaceous women, like his beloved Marita, in natural curvaceous settings."

Travis frowned. "What does your brother consider a natural curvaceous setting?"

"You know, curves found in nature, like on a gnarled pine tree. Or the stripes on the rocks along the shores of Georgian Bay. They've been washed smooth by the waves over time, exposing their curved lines. Have you seen them?"

"Not in person. But the Group of Seven painted in that part of the country, so of course I've seen their work," Travis said. "I've been to the Rockies, though."

"But the Rockies are hardly curvaceous," Angela exclaimed. "Not like the beautiful rocks of Georgian Bay."

"Okay, you've convinced me. One day I'll have to go there to see them."

"Maybe one day I'll take you there," Angela said, and then blushed. What a thing to say, for goodness sake! She was presuming that they would be together after the cruise. Which, of course, would never happen, according to Travis.

Luckily he didn't seem to notice her faux pas. He only responded jokingly, "I'll take you up on that!" and dropped the subject.

When they had finished viewing Murillo's home, it was time to return to the ship for lunch.

This time they sat together and discussed what they had seen in the morning. Angela leafed through her itinerary. "The Real Alcazar and the Cathedral are this afternoon. I'm beginning to think that's almost too much for one day."

Travis laughed. "What? Are you planning to stay behind again this afternoon to read your book?"

"I certainly am *not*," she said vehemently. "Even if I'll only remember a fraction of what I'll see this afternoon, I don't want to miss any of it."

"Good girl. You learn fast. So now should we sit in the lounge and finish our wine while we wait to board the bus?"

"I think I'd rather sit outside on the deck," Angela said, getting up. "It's too lovely to stay indoors."

Travis made a small courtly bow. "And I may join you?"

"*Ciertamente.*"

Travis frowned. "Are you trying to impress me with your Spanish, or throw me off track?"

Angela laughed. "Impress you, of course. Unless you're very easily confused." It was so nice to talk with him, with no need for formalities.

Outside a cool breeze blew in from the ocean, but she felt a cozy warmth inside her, just standing next to him.

In the afternoon the group explored the magnificent Real Alcazar palace.

"To think they began to build this over two thousand

years ago!" Angela exclaimed. "I can't even begin to imagine the work that must have gone into the architectural design and the construction."

"Yeah, and all these beautiful gardens that have been around for a few centuries," Travis said. "I find it difficult to fathom how anyone so long ago could have produced something so intricate and glorious as this." He sat down on a carved stone bench. "My own work feels so inadequate when I look at all this."

"I'm sure you're a very gifted designer yourself," Angela said.

Travis grimaced. "That's kind of you to say, but what do you know about me and my garden designs?"

"Well, as for your work, you must be good, or you wouldn't have been hired by the Italian firm to design their gardens," Angela countered. "Right?"

Travis chuckled. "Okay. I guess that's something to go on."

"And as for you, yourself, I think you are a very easy person to be with," she said and felt the heat rise to her cheeks. Was she getting too personal?

Travis got up and reached for her hand. "Thank you. That's the nicest thing I have heard in a long while and I sincerely return the compliment. Shall we catch up with the group?"

Hand in hand they walked through the English Garden, while Travis grumbled at not being able to take more time to admire it all.

Angela stood out on the deck after dinner, looking
up at the black night sky. Would the magic happen
again tonight? This whole trip was so different from
anything she had expected. She looked forward to each
new experience and found every moment delightful.
There was no doubt in her mind that it was because
of Travis. She couldn't imagine how any other travel
companion could have measured up to the enjoyment
she had in his company. She took a deep breath of the
clean evening air and then went inside.

She hoped she wasn't overdressed for the evening.
Contrary to her usual outfits, tonight she had put on
her black sleeveless dress a of very light fabric, with
spaghetti straps holding up the close-fitting top. The
skirt was full and flowing and she knew it would have
felt very elegant while dancing, swishing around her
legs and hips. But it seemed unlikely they would be
dancing tonight, for the program said they would be
treated to a Spanish dance performance.

In the lounge she was soon joined by Travis. He gave
a low, appreciative whistle and his eyebrows rose
quickly to show he liked what he saw. Angela blushed
and accepted his silent compliment without a word.
He seated himself beside her on a couch, and ordered
wine for them, while waiting for the evening's enter-

tainment to begin.

"I guess tonight *we* won't be doing much dancing," he said. "I must admit I would love to hold you in my arms and swirl you around, especially now that you're wearing that lovely dress."

"Thank you," Angela demurred, smiling with pleasure. "And I must admit I feel the same."

A moment later two Flamenco dancers stepped smartly onto the floor. The woman was dressed in a body-hugging flaming red dress with a flowing train while the man had on a dark, slim-fitting suit.

Clacking her castanets and tapping her heel, the woman enticed the man to join her, and soon they were engaged in a fiery dance that made Angela's pulse quicken. The guitar player who accompanied them strummed faster and faster, while the clicking of the castanets became more and more frenzied.

Travis blew a low whistle. "Wow! This sexy pair sure can get the pulse to speed up. Very talented."

Was he referring to the dancers or did he mean his own pulse? Of course Angela didn't ask, but her own heart was certainly beating much faster than normal.

"Yes, they are very talented," she said. And then, to give the performance a more pragmatic tone and to hide her own state of arousal, she added, "They have to be in superb condition to keep that up."

Sometime during the program Travis's arm came up

to the back of the couch behind her shoulders and rested there. She liked to feel his nearness and wished they could dance again like last night. The Flamenco entertainment went on for over an hour, with several other performers coming onto the floor strut their stuff and Angela feared there would be no time for dancing for her and Travis tonight.

Almost as if unawares, Travis slid his fingers lightly along her bare shoulders. When they touched her neck, a quick shiver coursed through her. Had he noticed?

He had. "Feeling chilly?" he asked.

"Oh, no, not at all." Angela gave a quick laugh. "How could I be chilly watching a hot performance like this?"

"That's what I was thinking. I wondered if you caught a cold out there on the deck last night." His twinkling eyes told her he didn't really think that was the case.

"No." She hadn't caught a cold. *En the contraria!* She'd caught something else. Something that made her blood flow faster in her veins and caused her pulse jump into overdrive. It was sexual desire, plain and simple.

Perhaps, Sylvia, she was *almost* ready to let her hair down . . .

At last the performers left, and the piano player sat at the keyboard.

"After that hot performance, I think you all are ready for something a bit more soothing," he joked.

He began a slow piece and immediately Travis got up. "May I?" he said with a slight bow and Angela rose, happy that she had decided to pack the black dress into her suitcase. It had been an impulsive move, and she had fully expected never to wear it during the cruise. Now she was happy she had taken it, for the flowing skirts swishing against her legs felt sexy and luxurious.

As they danced Travis held her close but every now and then, holding her with one hand, he made her take a turn on her own, which made the full skirts swirl around her legs.

He ran his hand down her back, fingering the fabric of her dress. "I hope you don't mind me saying that this really feels sexy," he said with a mischievous twinkle in his eyes. "After that performance and now your sexy dress . . . Whew!"

"Don't start getting any ideas, young man," Angela said, laughing. But she couldn't deny that she had the very same thoughts.

Travis looked dejected. "Too late. The ideas are there already."

"And there let them stay," Angela said and to give her words more emphasis, she gave him a small push with her palm.

Though she would much rather have pulled him closer.

The bus climbed slowly up the Rock to the Gibraltar Nature Reserve, taking the excited tourists to visit the colony of Barbary macaque monkeys. As on the previous day, Travis had joined Angela and again sat beside her. This morning he hadn't even asked if he could join her, but after sitting with her at breakfast, he'd simply climbed onto the bus behind her and sat down, as though it were the most natural thing in the world.

Angela could tell the other passengers thought they were a "pair". And truly she wouldn't have minded if it remained that way for the rest of the voyage. Travis was such a nice person to be with, to talk with, and to exchange views with. Neither had asked about the other's plans after the cruise ended in Barcelona, and somehow Angela was loathe to probe. If it was true what Travis had said about people never keeping in touch after a trip, then these few days were all they had. No matter how well they "hit it off".

It was a depressing thought, but instead of letting it spoil the day, Angela decided to do another Scarlett O'Hara and not think about it today. And not even tomorrow, if she could help it. Instead she would follow Sylvia's advice and perhaps let down her hair a little. After all, if she enjoyed being with Travis and this was all they would ever have, why not enjoy it? To the fullest, if it came to that.

Travis leaned past Angela to look out the bus window. "I wonder when we'll start seeing those infamous little critters."

Just then the bus driver made an announcement. "If you look out to your right, you can see a family sitting on the rocks beyond the barricade. A family of monkeys, I mean." The driver chuckled at his own joke while the passengers laughed. "Remember you are not allowed to feed them," he went on. "They aren't hungry, because they are fed regularly each day. But they're greedy little devils and they'll reach into any purse or backpack that's left open, so keep your valuables safe from them. We'll be stopping in a couple of minutes. Have fun and take lots of pictures."

The bus emptied onto the roadside and in no time they were surrounded by monkeys of every size. Angela laughed as Travis played with a baby monkey that climbed onto his back and then tried to steal the wallet from his back pocket.

"Hey you little pick-pocket!" Travis cried. "I'm going to tell your parents you're on your way to a life of crime." He removed the baby from his back and hoisted him onto the barricade that prevented tourists from going over the edge. "What's that you say? Your daddy's the biggest thief in the whole pack? Well, in that case I guess you're just learning the family business."

All the tourists around her were snapping photos, which reminded Angela she hadn't taken any of Travis in the three days they'd been together. What would she have to remember him by, if the only images of him she had were in her mind.

Another little monkey had jumped onto Travis's shoulders and Angela snapped a photo of the two of them. She then approached a nearby tourist and held out her iPhone. "Would you mind taking a picture of my friend and me?" she asked, and then called to Travis. "Come here for a picture with me, please."

Travis came and, putting his arm around her shoulders, he pulled her against his side. "Gotta strike a romantic pose here," he said. And then, without warning, he turned her face toward him and kissed her. It was a long, deep kiss that sent her heart tumbling down over the precipice overlooking the city.

She didn't resist. Instead she put her arms around his neck and kissed him back, while the grinning photographer kept snapping shots.

"Whew!" Travis at last said and released her. "I was just posing for a photo. What's your excuse?"

The photographer laughed and handed the camera back to Angela who turned away from Travis so he wouldn't see how the kiss had caused her face to become flushed. "I just wanted a memento of this day," she threw over her shoulder. "Your romantic posing was a bit excessive, don't you think?" She thanked the man, while feeling totally dismayed at the thought that Travis might have misread her response to his kiss. She had simply played along with him.

"Well, it sure felt like you were posing right along with me," Travis remarked with a grin. "And very convincingly, too." He then bent over to chat with the monkey that still hung around his legs. "Come back into my arms, you little munchkin. My lady-love just deserted me."

Angela gave a little laugh to hide her dismay. It was obvious that, like a goofy kid, Travis had only been acting in front of the camera, while she had foolishly allowed her heart to soar, reacting to the kiss as though it was something special and significant.

"May I see the pics?" Travis asked and Angela handed him her iPhone.

"Hey, there are no monkeys in these pictures!" he exclaimed. "How will you remember where they were taken?"

"Oh, don't worry. I have one of you and the baby monkey that will refresh my memory," she replied and tucked the iPhone back into her purse. She had to make a valiant effort to be light-hearted like he was, and not take things seriously as she always tended to do. Just because Travis hadn't reacted to the kiss like she had, was no reason to be dismayed.

After a tour of the caves and tunnels that were built during WWII, the bus took them back to the ship to rest and get freshened up before dinner. Then, while they were eating, the ship hoisted anchor and left the Rock, heading for Granada.

As they entered the lounge, the piano player was again warming up his fingers to get everyone dancing. Travis went to get them some wine and for a few numbers they sat at a small table, watching the few couples who ventured onto the dance floor.

When the piano player started to play a Latin number, Travis stood up and made a courtly bow in front of Angela. "Señorita? The last time we didn't dare to try this, but are you up for it now?"

Angela laughed, knowing he was referring to all the champagne she had consumed on her birthday. This time she rose and soon surrendered to the fast-pulsing rhythms. Travis was a superb dancer and a great leader and she found herself following him effortlessly.

"I didn't know I could dance Latin numbers," she marveled. Was it because of the fast rhythm, or was dancing with Travis making her sound slightly breathless?

"Well, you sure dance like a pro," Travis said, and twirled her around. "I've taken years of lessons. What's your excuse?"

"I guess I'm just a natural born dancer," Angela boasted. This was fun! She felt almost as light-headed as she had on her birthday night after consuming the champagne. Just then she stumbled. "Or not!" She giggled.

"Don't worry, you haven't shattered my image of you as Ginger Rogers," Travis comforted her.

"And, so far you have not shattered my image of you," Angela riposted. "As a fine travel companion."

She frowned as a cloud seemed to pass over his face. But a grin followed so quickly she thought she had to have been mistaken.

"Not as Fred Astaire?" he quipped.

"Hm . . . Pretty close to that, I must admit."

He twirled her around a few times. "I'll just have to keep working on it."

When the dance was over, Travis removed his arm from around her and they clapped. They were about to return to their seats when a slow number started and instead of leading her to their table Travis pulled her against himself.

"Let's dance this one, too." His voice husky and without waiting for an answer, he began to walk slowly in rhythm, holding her waist with both hands. She put her hands around his neck and they began to slowly sway as one. Neither spoke. Travis bent his head and softly nuzzled her neck, making delicious tremors trickled down her body. And then, as the music swooned to a crescendo, he kissed her, taking her mouth possessively, deeply. It wasn't just a kiss, it was ecstasy. Her legs went soft under her and she was afraid she would collapse right there on the dance floor.

"We mustn't," Angela stammered weakly when she was able to speak again. "People can see us."

"Then we must go where people can't see."

Angela floated in a trance, her hand is his, as they walked outside and continued along the deck. Twice today he had kissed her and both times the strong reaction inside her had caught her off guard. His kisses had been pure mind-blowing, fantasy-fulfilling delight and she couldn't help it if her wanton body wanted more. She simply had to see what else was in store for her. They reached the same spot as before, where the lights of the deck lamps didn't reach, and she melted against him, eager to have his lips on hers again.

Travis kissed her and she responded with abandon. As his kisses became deeper, more dizzying, she realized this could very easily lead to something much more intimate. His hands explored her body, and Angela had to force down a whimper of want that rose from deep inside her. The night was turning into something unreal. Was this Brigadoon? Was this the magic fairyland? And was it only two days ago they had met? It felt like she had known him forever.

Her head spun crazily. His animal magnetism was drowning her good senses and she knew if she didn't slow things down, she would do something totally non-Angelic. Like fall into bed with a man she hardly knew.

In the nick of time her common sense kicked in and she whispered, "We should go in."

Travis nodded. "Right," he said hoarsely.

They re-entered the lounge, and sat down at their table. He signaled the waiter to bring them more wine, and when it arrived, he raised his glass.

"To us," he said and looked deep into her eyes.

To us? What did that mean? "Us" had no place on these voyages. At least not a long-term kind of "us". And definitely not a forever kind of "us".

"To us as long as we are on this cruise," she responded, to get the words into the correct perspective.

"Precisely," he agreed. "I consider myself extremely lucky to have found you on board this ship. Imagine if I hadn't. With whom would I be spending this magical evening?" he reached for her hand and gave it a gentle squeeze. "Nobody. There is no one on board that I would want to spend my time with."

"Really?" she asked, raising her eyebrows. "No one?"

"No one," he assured her and then asked, slight dismay in his voice, "Why? Is there someone else you would rather spend your evenings with? I just selfishly assumed you felt the same as—"

"Oh, of course I feel the same!" Angela hurried to explain. "I wouldn't want to spend my time with anyone else, either!"

Travis sighed. "Whew! You had me worried there for a while, I thought I would have to relinquish my seat on the bus to someone else."

Angela laughed. "No worries! Your seat is safe, as long as you don't start to demand the window seat."

"Never, if that's a condition. Besides, you are the one who takes more pictures, so the window seat is yours."

The evening wore on and they danced far into the night, again being the last couple to leave the lounge. Toward the end the tired piano player only played slow pieces, so they didn't even bother to return to their table between numbers. They simply stood there, arms around each other, waiting for the next piece, his body telling her he wanted her, just as she wanted him. Angela recalled someone saying that dancing was like making love standing up, and that was exactly what they were doing, but not once did he indicate he expected her to go to bed with him. Except with his body.

"I think we should let the poor piano player go to bed," Angela at last said.

"You're right." Travis took her hand and led her down to her cabin door. There he kissed her—deeply and thoroughly—and turned to go.

Angela, her head buzzing with wine and his kisses, didn't know if she would have invited him in had he given her the slightest signal that he was thinking of it. And that certainly would have been totally out of character for her.

She smiled to herself as she closed the cabin door. She hadn't exactly let her hair down, but had certainly loosened it up quite a bit.

Okay, Sylvia, are you happy now?

Travis's goodnight kisses still tingled on her lips and she could still feel his hands caressing her, even as she prepared for bed. Tomorrow they would be in Granada. Angela glanced at the clock on the night table and smiled. *Today* they would be in Granada. She only knew Granada from the words of a song, but it sounded like the most romantic place on earth. Just where she wanted to visit after tonight.

"*And when day is done and the sun starts to set in Granada. . .*" she hummed and took a few faltering dance steps around the cabin while waving around her silk pajama top like a banner. Who cared if Brigadoon would disappear in a few days, because right now she was happy. Happy and carefree. She couldn't remember feeling like this ever before in her life.

Because the ship was now in the Straight of Gibraltar, getting ready to enter the Mediterranean Sea, there were no more Atlantic swells to worry about. But Angela didn't trust the conditions, and decided to take a pill for motion sickness, just in case. She didn't want anything to spoil her dreams tonight.

Chapter Three

Travis couldn't sleep. He knew he had carried this thing with Angela much farther than he had intended. In fact, he'd had no intention of starting any "thing" with her at all. He had simply wanted to have the company of this beautiful woman during the voyage. The first evening when he saw her sitting there alone, reading her book, he'd been attracted to her. But she had looked rather too aloof. So much aloof, in fact, that he had decided against going over to speak to her. Instead he had gone to his cabin to fetch his drawing pad and pencil, and had proceeded to sketch her portrait.

She was a true beauty, with her dark hair drawn into a tight bun at the back of her slender, elegant neck. When she bent it to read, it made him think of a black swan. He had decided she looked rather Spanish, which had turned out to be a correct assumption.

Her large, dark eyes—which he had only glimpsed when she'd occasionally raised her head—were doe-shaped.

But why was she traveling alone, not accompanied by a friend? Was she nursing some broken relationship? Or was she getting over some other sad event in her life?

Like he was.

Although, surprisingly, Elaine's death just over three weeks ago hadn't hit him very hard, nor made him sad, like it should have. It had merely been the final epoch of her agonizing journey with the increasingly worsening disease. It had been as though he had packed a suitcase for an old friend and sent her off on a voyage, never to return. Once the funeral and the ensuing paperwork were over, it was like they had never been married. They had no children and the in-laws were long departed. After Elaine's illness progressed to the point where she had to be institutionalized, he'd had no dealings with her siblings or their progeny for several years. Not until the funeral. Their visits to the nursing home had seldom coincided with his, so seeing them at the funeral had been almost awkward. Handshakes, hugs and meaningless air kisses.

During the long years when he had dutifully visited her each week, Elaine and he had never quarreled. Except when she had angrily told him to stop coming.

"I want you to stay away. Don't come back any more," she had said in her thick, garbled voice. "There's nothing left of me any more. The only part that still looks normal are my fingers."

Which is why she always had the nursing staff keep them carefully manicured and lacquered with bright nail polish so she could—with difficulty—bring them up to see as she lay on her back in bed.

She'd even told him to get a divorce and start a new life. "I'm never going to get out of this bed," she had stated with no self-pity in her voice. "You must not slowly die with me. I'm not your wife any longer."

But Travis had remained faithful to her, never going on a date or giving more than a passing thought to other women or to sex.

Until this voyage.

So, what was going on now? Was it because he was—technically—no longer being unfaithful to Elaine, so there was nothing preventing him from kissing Angela? Or was it because after all the long years of abstinence, with the floodgates now open, he was in danger of falling overboard?

Or was there something else? Was he attracted to Angela for her own qualities? Which were . . . what? What exactly did he know about her? That she was beautiful. That she had a gentle sense of humour. That they got along well. But he knew it was easy to get along well with a person when you had been together only three days. How would they get along after seven days? After seven years?

Whoa! His mind was getting slightly ahead of the game. If he still found her attractive when the voyage was over, perhaps they could keep in touch, even though he had little hope of that happening. While traveling he had met many interesting, fascinating people, both men and women, but had never kept in touch with any of them longer than a month or two. After the promised photos had been exchanged, things had always dwindled down to maybe the odd Christmas card for a couple of years. Usually nothing.

Travis clicked off the bedside lamp. The thought of losing contact forever with Angela produced an odd sensation in his chest, right where his heart was. It was a feeling he hadn't experienced for a long time. Not since the early days with Elaine, when he had been madly in love and had wanted to be with her every minute of every day.

But of course he was not in love with Angela. He couldn't be. He didn't believe in that love at first sight crap. But still the thought of losing touch with her at the end of this trip didn't sit well with him.

What he wanted to do was kiss her again. And have her right here beside him in bed. And hold her slender body against him as he had done on the dance floor.

But he knew that wasn't love. That was just normal sexual attraction.

Day four dawned bright and sunny like every morning on the trip had done, and just like she did every morning, Angela jumped out of bed and ran to open her Juliet balcony doors. The ship had docked at Montril sometime during the night or early morning hours, and down on the dock, she could see the bus already waiting for them, ready to carry them to Granada.

Excitement built up inside her during breakfast. She had such high expectations for this day that she could hardly eat. "*Granada, I'm falling under your spell . . .*" she hummed in her head as she sipped her coffee.

"We won't be back on the ship for lunch today," Travis told her. "So you better eat up, or pay handsomely at a restaurant for your meal."

"Oh, I won't mind paying," Angela assured him. "It'll be nice to take in some local food for a change."

"Great. Maybe you'll even treat me?" Travis looked at her, blinking with Hush Puppy eyes.

Angela laughed. "Or maybe not."

They boarded the bus and soon it was filled with enthusiastic passengers, all anxious to experience the famed Granada.

Alhambra Palace, on top of a hill overlooking the city of Granada, was even more wonderful than Angela had expected. She had read somewhere it was like "a pearl set in emeralds", and this description proved accurate. She found the intricately carved ceiling decorations enchantingly beautiful—like layers upon layers of white lace. Travis admired the Court of the Lions where the statues of the twelve beasts symbolized strength and power. And as they walked among the fountains, flowing water channels, and the reflecting pools, Travis couldn't stop commenting on the beauty of it all.

"They sure had some very talented landscape designers," he remarked shaking his head.

"And to think they probably never even went to an art school," Angela added.

"Maybe they did," Travis said. "Who knows what kinds of schools they had in those days. But I've never seen anything about that mentioned anywhere in my readings."

In the endless gardens the flowerbeds glowed in the mid-morning sunlight. At one point, through their earphones, they heard a magnificent tenor voice praising the beauty of Granada.

"Granada", Angela breathed. "I have heard that song countless times, but it has never sounded as meaningful and beautiful as now. Here I am, amid all the loveliness he is singing about."

Travis took her hand as they strolled slowly along the flower-bordered path. It was almost too beautiful to bear and tears welled up in Angela's eyes. "I am totally enthralled by the beauty of this place," she whispered. "I don't know when I have felt this happy. I don't ever want this to end."

Travis shrugged. "Brigadoon," he said almost carelessly. "It will soon disappear."

Offended by his dismissive tone, Angela pulled her hand away. "Oh, please don't say it like that! That's cruel."

"Sorry. It's just that everything has to end."

Why was he so ready and willing to think about the end of everything? Just like on their first night they had talked about how everything would evaporate, like Brigadoon. How all relationships formed on travels would end the moment they walked down the gangplank for the last time. Perhaps he was simply being realistic since he had traveled a lot and knew from experience what would happen, but still she couldn't help being disappointed.

All right. Maybe she was just being too sentimental about these things. Probably that was something she should be guarding against. Yes, pragmatism was what she should be practising instead of getting all weepy-eyed over some romantic experience.

They walked past a white stucco wall where bright red bougainvillea cascaded down, almost reaching the cobblestone streets. Aiming for a touch of light-heartedness, Angela stopped under the flowers and struck a pose.

"How would you like to take a picture of this Spanish señorita underneath those lovely bougainvillea?" she quipped,

"Beautiful!" Travis exclaimed. He reached for the camera in his back pocket. "But first, let down your hair. Let it cascade down your shoulders like the bougainvillea above you."

Angela laughed, slightly embarrassed. "Really?"

"Please."

Pulling a face, she removed the pins that held the bun at the back of her head and let her black hair flow to her shoulders.

"That's it," Travis said. "Now look at me. Pretend I'm your lover."

Heat rushed to her cheeks. Pretend he was her lover? That wasn't difficult to do, considering she'd been dreaming about him every night. She looked at him and felt her eyes mist.

"You're lovely," he whispered.

The camera clicked, but for a moment neither of them moved.

"Okay. I think that was a great shot," Travis said abruptly and slipped the camera back into his pocket. "No one will believe me when I say the woman in the picture is Canadian and doesn't live in Spain."

"May I see it?" Angela asked. "I'd like to make sure I

don't look too silly."

Travis dug out the camera and handed it to her. Angela was surprised at the expression on her face. Her eyes were slightly dewy and her whole face glowed. Without a word she closed the camera and gave it back to him. Had her face revealed too much? Would he be to able to read in her expression how she felt about him? Because she definitely had developed feelings for him—feelings she didn't want to explore in broad daylight.

She quickly pushed her hair back up into its usual tight bun and neither of them said much as they walked on. The bus was ready for boarding and as soon as the last straggler was on, they headed toward the Royal Chapel of Granada.

Angela stood silently before the tombs of King Ferdinand and Queen Isabella. "I have read that they were a loving couple. I think it is beautiful that they are together even in death."

Behind her she heard Travis snort. "What's so beautiful about death? There's just a couple of skeletons inside those tombs, no matter how nicely they are carved."

Incredulously Angela turned to look at him. "Is that how you feel about death?"

"I don't feel anything about death. It's just the end of life, that's all. You're packed into a box and sent on your way. Much like taking off on a trip, only you never return. I don't see why people want to romanticize it."

Disappointment filled her. Was he really this cold and unfeeling? "I'm sorry you feel that way."

"No reason to be sorry." His voice was dismissive. "Just because some carver five hundred years ago made those beautiful tombs, it doesn't change the fact that inside them are two dead bodies. Or what's left of them."

"If that's how you feel, then . . ." Angela shrugged. "That's how you feel." She turned and started to walk toward the exit. "I'll wait for you outside. I think I've had enough of all this."

But Travis caught up with her and took her by the arm. "I didn't mean to offend you," he said, sounding penitent. "I'm sorry if I sounded blunt. It's just that I'm not into this idolizing of death."

Angela pulled her arm away. "I have no reason to be offended. You're a pragmatist, I'm a romantic. You think the way you do and I think the way I do."

"So how is your thinking different?" Travis asked.

"In a way that you'd probably find quite morbid," Angela replied.

"Tell me. I want to know."

They continued to walk side by side and Travis reached for her hand. She didn't pull it away. Instead she decided to do as he had asked, and tell him what he wanted to know, all the while knowing he would more than likely be repulsed by it.

"We celebrate and honour our loved ones who are dead on Dia de Muerto. That is Day of the Dead," she began. "We look on death as the next step in our lives, not the end and believe that the souls of the dead return to join their families for the festivities. We go to the cemetery to clean the graves and create a shrine where we place incense, fruit, flowers and candles. We tell stories about our grandparents and great-grandparents, whatever my mother remembers about them. When we were small, my brother Miguel and I got treats called *calaveras de azúcar* which were skulls made from sugar. They symbol-ize death and the afterlife."

Angela stopped and turned to look at Travis and gauge his reaction. She was surprised not to see dis-gust or shock in his eyes.

"Your family does all that?" he asked. "Even in Canada?"

"Yes. In our family those traditions have survived even in Canada. We are taught to remember our family members who have passed on."

For a few minutes Travis was silent. "When do you hold this celebration?" he then asked.

"The beginning of November," she replied. "It hap-pens to fall close to Hallowe'en, but doesn't really have anything to do with it."

"I'll have to remember that," he said.

Angela was surprised at the pensive tone in his words but decided against probing. She continued to walk down the hill toward the waiting bus and Travis fell in step beside her.

"Listen, I don't want us to argue," he said. "I really would like to spend the rest of this trip with you."

Angela stopped again and turned to look at him. "What's the difference? We'll be in Barcelona soon and that will be the end of it. What does it matter when we part?"

"It matters to me. We're not disembarking for another two days yet. A lot can happen in two days."

"Such as . . .?" She turned to head down the hill again.

Travis took a hop to catch up with her. "Well, for one thing we could fall in love." He walked backwards in front of her. "That's what people do on cruise ships in the movies."

Angela suppressed a smile. She found his boyish enthusiasm endearing and despite herself her mood lightened. "This isn't a movie, Travis. Real live people don't fall in love on cruise ships."

Travis grabbed her by the waist and twirled her around. "Let's break tradition," he cried. "Let's you and I fall in love against all odds."

His frivolity was contagious. "Okay," she said. "Tonight after dinner we'll fall in love." She disengaged herself when she saw people by the bus smiling at them.

"Why not before dinner?" Travis asked.

"It might spoil my appetite," she shot at him.

Travis roared with laughter. "Well, thanks a lot! And you just told me you're a romantic."

"I was, but you cured me of it," she riposted.

"Just when you made me into one," he exclaimed and again pulled her close to him.

Although she wanted to resist and move away, she didn't. He was right, they only had two days.

Most of the next day was spent at sea, so Angela and Travis took walks on the deck under the Mediterranean sun.

"Do you know how to play double solitaire?" Angela asked when they had returned to the lounge after a walk.

Travis signaled the waiter. "I didn't know you play solitaire."

"When I was living with my mother, I played it often," Angela said, and then, for some reason, found it necessary to add, "But I'm not living with my mother anymore."

"Oh? And how come you aren't living with your

mother anymore?" Travis asked, and Angela realized they hadn't shared anything about their lives outside the ship. Other than telling him her brother was an artist and had twin sons, she hadn't said much about her family.

The waiter had brought them glasses of wine and as she sipped hers, she filled Travis in on how Miguel and Marita with their babies had moved in to live with mother, so Angela was now free to live on her own.

"So do you have a deck of cards?" she asked and drew her own out of her purse.

"I'll ask the waiter to being me one," Travis said.

A few minutes later, he shuffled his deck and, out of the blue, asked, "And after this trip you're moving in with your boyfriend, I suppose?"

Angela had to laugh. She knew he was fishing for information, but decided not to supply any. "No, I don't think so," she said, purposely leaving it open to speculation. Besides, he hadn't volunteered to tell her about himself, either. And she wasn't about to ask. After all, what was the point? They were parting after the cruise, never to see each other again, so why should she know anything about his life? Or about his girlfriends. She was pretty sure he didn't have a wife, because there was no ring. But who knew? Rings were easy enough to remove and many men simply didn't wear one.

"What's his name?" Travis asked, while he spread out his cards.

"What's your girlfriend's name?" Angela answered playfully with a question and began to play, having beat him at the deal.

For a few minutes neither spoke as they concentrated on the game, trying to get as many of their cards into the centre piles as possible.

"At the moment I don't have one," Travis at last said when there was a lull in the hectic pace.

Angela's heart skipped a beat and she swallowed. Since it seemed neither of them had a significant other at home, why shouldn't they keep in touch after this trip was over? But *she* certainly wasn't going to suggest anything. He was the one who knew how things worked on trips and conferences.

Travis moved the Queen of Hearts onto the King of Clubs. "Do you really think I'd be playing cards with you if I had a girlfriend waiting for me?" He grinned. "Or kissing you?"

"I would hope not." She really did hope, because otherwise he would be a two-timing cad.

"So can I hope the same about you?" he continued his probing.

"I can't continue," she murmured, hoping to distract him. "Can you?"

"No, it doesn't look like it," Travis said, flipping his

remaining cards into the air. "So who's the winner?"

Angela picked up the piles of cards in the centre and sorted them out. "I am," she announced. "No need even to count. I can tell there's more of my cards here."

"I concede," Travis said. "So what's your reply?"

"To . . .?" Of course she knew, but didn't want to expose her lack of a boyfriend.

"To my earlier question, of course. Do you have someone waiting in the wings?"

She couldn't hide the facts any longer. "No," she said quietly. "I don't."

Travis put out his hand to cover hers and gave it a gentle squeeze. "Good."

He looked directly into her eyes. Angela felt a rush of heat on her face and had to lower her head so he wouldn't see her blush.

"Listen, we're going to be docking at Ibiza soon. Did you want to take the bus to tour the salt flats?"

Angela hesitated. "Umm . . . that doesn't really sound too interesting to me. But seeing the medieval fortification would be—"

"Let's not go," he rasped, his voice thick.

Her pulse beat a rapid tattoo. "What should we do instead?" she asked quietly, although there was no mistaking his meaning. "Of course there's the whole afternoon . . ."

The ship docked at Ibiza with all the accompanying hustle and bustle on the docks, while hand in hand Angela and Travis headed for his cabin. Her heart hammered so loudly she was sure he could hear. He unlocked the cabin door and held it open for her. The most obvious piece of furniture in the small room was, of course, the queen bed and Angela couldn't avoid seeing it no matter how she tried to look elsewhere.

"Nice room," she croaked. Sure! Her larynx had to let her down just when she wanted to appear suave and worldly.

She coughed and tried again. "Love the view," she quipped and was able to muster a modicum of humour into the voice. This side of the boat faced the docks where the scurrying, shouting dock hands were pulling on the heavy cables, getting the ship attached.

"Great, isn't it?" Travis said and went to pull the curtains shut, hiding the activity from view.

The closed curtains created a sense of intimacy that sent a shiver of expectation through Angela's body.

"My cabin is on the other side of the boat so my view is probably a bit nicer," she said, keeping up the banter to hide her nervousness. "Besides, I'm on an upper deck."

"Maybe tomorrow we can look out your window and compare."

Angela gulped. Was he really planning to do this

again tomorrow? What if things didn't work out well between them this afternoon? He was committing himself to another tryst tomorrow without first making sure they were compatible?

Travis moved to a small fridge. "Would you like a drink? Unfortunately all I have here is some white wine." He pulled out a bottle.

"Yes, thank you." It was still early in the afternoon, but . . .

Travis unscrewed the cap and poured them each a drink.

He raised his glass and looked at her over the rim. "Here's to the start of a beautiful friendship," he said, mimicking Bogart in *Casablanca*.

"I thought beautiful friendships on a ship never last," Angela said.

His eyes were almost black when he looked at her. "There are always exceptions," he murmured.

"Are there?" she whispered.

"I believe there are." He put his glass on a side table and stepped close to her. "If one really wants it." His voice was low, enticing, letting her know he wanted her to be the exception.

Her heart was beating so hard it was making the hand holding the wine glass shake.

Of course he noticed. He took the glass from her and placed it on the table next to his and took her by the shoulders. "Angela, you are so lovely," he said softly and bent his head to nuzzle her neck. "Please take your hair down."

Yes, that was exactly what she wanted to do! She reached up and unpinned the bun at the back of her neck, letting her long, dark hair flow down onto her shoulders.

"Lovely," he whispered and ran his fingers through the locks. "You should always wear it like this."

Angela felt strangely exposed. Almost as if she had shed her clothes. She smiled uncomfortably. "I don't think I'd like—"

"You're right," Travis said. "I wouldn't like it either. It makes you look much too sexy and every man on the ship would be after you."

She laughed. "You are being silly. I don't believe this would have any effect on anyone. It's just hair."

He continued to play with the long strands. "Oh, but it would. Your hair is so silky smooth. Just running my fingers through it is already having a very strong effect on me." He put his arms around her and pulled her against him. "A very strong effect." And then he kissed her.

Angela could easily feel the strong effect he was re-ferring to and her body responded in kind.

This was it, Sylvia! Her hair was down, literally, and she would find out what resulted from that.

Chapter Four

Travis picked her up in his arms and held her mouth with his lips as he carried her the few feet to the bed that was waiting for them. It was the first time in seven years he was holding a woman with the express intent of making love. He was surprised how natural it felt, as though he'd had sex regularly in all those long, intervening years. And he was surprised, also, that the thought of Elaine caused him no guilt as he began to undress the beautiful woman lying on his bed. But, then, as his hands touched her soft bare skin, all thought of everything and anyone else vanished from his brain.

He divested her of her blouse and bra, and then kissed her firm breasts. Sucking on the puckered nipples sent him over the moon. It was so exquisitely wonderful to be making love to a woman at long last. It was as though he had found the Golden Chalice.

"Angela," he whispered. "I want you so much." He

was rewarded with a soft whimper that told him she was feeling the same desire.

She murmured softly and moved under him in a way that let him know she was ready for him. He pulled off the rest of her outer clothing, and then let his eyes feast on the silky, lace panties that barely covered her mound.

He kissed her navel and then let his mouth slide down. His tongue felt the silky lace and then slipped into her groove.

He heard her gasp and then she opened her thighs for him, letting him know she found this pleasurable. For a few moments he allowed himself to kiss her through the panty, but when she began to thrust herself at him, he quickly removed them and let his tongue work on her without the obstacle of the fabric. Her gasps changed to moans and then, with a small shriek of pleasure, she climaxed.

He allowed her breathing to calm down before getting up and reaching for their wine glasses.

"What are we drinking to now?" Angela asked. She sat up and wound the bed sheet around herself. Her face was still flushed and her dark hair disheveled. She had never looked more beautiful to him.

He sat on the bed beside her. "Let's drink to the beauty of love."

"Yes . . . let's," she said, but the hesitation in her

voice told him she wasn't absolutely certain about it.

They touched glasses.

"Didn't you find that beautiful?" he asked.

She took a sip of her wine. "Yes, I did, but I don't know if I would call it love."

"What would you call it?"

"I would call it love-making. Wouldn't you?"

"Well, perhaps technically, but we wouldn't be doing this if there weren't some feeling between us. Some beautiful feeling, which I choose to call love."

She hesitated again. "I don't think I would go that far . . . "

He quickly gulped down his wine and put his glass on the table. "So what would you call it?" The woman was honest and thoughtful and didn't take things lightly. He liked that about her.

"Attraction. I think I would call it sexual attraction," Angela said.

"Yes, I agree. Beautiful sexual attraction. And I think we shouldn't waste any more time. We only have to-morrow."

His words hung in the air between them. Her dark eyes suddenly looked sad, and inside him there was a strange jab of pain. Only tomorrow.

He reached for her and, holding her tightly against him, kissed her. Again and again his hungry mouth ravaged her, and she responded in kind. In no time he had removed his own clothing and her hands were caressing his body, exploring, exciting, drawing a groan from deep inside him.

But then she stopped. Breathing hard, he raised his head to look down at her face.

"Do you have protection?" she asked, her voice raspy with emotion.

He managed a smile. "Would you believe, this ship has a pretty well stocked pharmacy."

She put her palms against his chest and, with a frown, tried to push him off. "You planned this?"

But he didn't release her. "No. I didn't exactly *plan* this. But you can't blame a guy for dreaming, hoping that you might want . . ." He raised her chin and looked into her dark eyes. "You *did* want this, too, didn't you?"

He barely heard her. "Yes," she whispered.

At her reply relief washed over him. He reached for his pants and found a packet in one of the pockets. The last time he had sex it was Elaine who had been using protection. He hoped to God he still remembered from his bachelor days how to put on a condom smoothly, without looking awkward.

But Angela took the package from him. "I have never done this," she said, smiling. "But I want to do it now."

He lay on his back on the bed and just the thought of her handling him quickly brought him to a full erection.

She tore open the package and slipped the condom on him. The process was so simple, so natural, than he needn't have worried.

Then she surprised him by climbing on top of him and, sitting astride, inserted him inside her. She settled down on him and began to move.

"Tell me what feels good," she said. "I have never done this before, either."

"Oh, baby, anything you do feels good," Travis breathed. After years of celibacy, simply being inside a woman felt beyond wonderful.

In short order her quick movements brought him to a climax. After his breathing had settled down, she came to lie beside him and caressed his chest with her palms.

"I bet you go to a gym," she said with a small laugh, kissing his shoulders and pecs.

Travis couldn't help feeling proud. "Yeah," he admitted with an embarrassed chuckle. "Guilty as charged." He did, indeed, go to gym twice a week and knew his body showed it.

"Then you're in such a good shape that in no time at all you will be ready for another round?" Angela teased him and gave his nipple a tiny bite.

Her complete freedom and gentle teasing were like an aphrodisiac. That she surrendered herself to him so freely filled him with awe, completely beguiling him.

He wanted to hold her in his arms forever.

Her teasing nibbles and caresses soon had the desired effect. He kissed her lips until she moaned under him and opened her thighs to grip him close with her legs.

"Travis," she whispered. "Please." Her voice was hoarse.

He quickly sheathed himself again and then entered her in one quick move.

She gasped sharply and then whimpered in her need for him. He set a rhythm that quickly brought her to a climax. As spasms racked her body, he groaned and joined her, thrusting wildly. When it was over, she lay in his arms, panting, while his breathing gradually slowed down.

"That was wonderful," he murmured against her hair. "Beyond wonderful. It was over the moon and back."

"Yes, it was," she whispered.

He looked down at her glowing face. Her lips were still lusciously swollen from the passionate kissing and her dark eyes were bright with satisfaction. He wanted to remember her exactly as she looked at this moment.

He got up and got his camera from the top of the dresser. "May I please take a picture of you?" he asked. "You are too lovely for words."

She rose onto her hands and knees, tucking her feet

under her, and before she had time to become embarrassed or change her expression, he snapped several shots of her.

"I need to have this reminder of our time together," he said, and was immediately sorry for his choice of words. Her face lost its glow and her eyes clouded over.

"I guess you should send me a copy, too, so I will not forget," she said flippantly and sat on the side of the bed. "You know what you said about exchanging a few photos and—"

"I didn't mean to sound like I would ever forget this," he hurried to explain, but it was too late. He saw moisture in her eyes and could have kicked himself for spoiling their wonderful moment. He sat down beside her and put an arm around her shoulders. "Angela, I will never forget. This will be my most treasured memory."

She looked up at him, her face skeptical. "Of this trip."

"Of my life," he said and pulled her close against him. "Of my life. There can never be anything more wonderful than this day with you."

"Yes, you say that now, but on your next trip you will meet someone more wonderful and tell her the same thing." She said it, not bitterly, but like it was a simple fact.

He turned her face to him and kissed her. He wanted

to tell her he had never had an affair before. An affair? This wasn't an affair because now he was a widower.

So why didn't he tell her? Why didn't he say that before this cruise he had never had sex with anyone because he'd had a wife. But then he would also have to tell her that Elaine had died recently. Which he couldn't do because he knew what her reaction would be. She would be shocked to learn he was making love to another woman so soon after his wife's funeral. Even telling her about the seven years when Elaine and he hadn't really been husband and wife wouldn't help. Telling her that Elaine had lived in an institution and that he had faithfully gone to see her despite her insistence that he stop the visits, despite her pleas that he divorce her and get a life—he knew even that wouldn't carry much weight against the all too recent funeral.

Because somehow he knew Angela was the kind of woman who would be repelled by the thought that he'd jumped into bed with a woman before his wife's body had barely cooled down. No matter what the circumstances. So he said nothing.

Angela disengaged herself from his arms and got up. Silently she reached for her clothes and slowly began to get dressed. Travis sat on the bed and watched, feeling more depressed than he had ever been in his life. After just having had the most wonderful experience of his life with this woman, it was over.

She finished dressing but instead of leaving, she stood, absently fingering a few items on the dresser. He sensed she was reluctant to leave, and was looking for answers.

"I meant what I said. This really is the most wonderful thing that ever happened to me," he said earnestly.

She turned her head slightly to look at him. "Really?"

"Really. Please believe me, Angela." His voice was pleading. She had to believe him. She could not end this and leave.

He could tell she was relenting, for a small smile played on her lips as she continued to stand there, fingering the objects on the dresser. Casually she picked up his key ring and looked at it more closely.

Travis froze. He'd forgotten that on the ring was a photo of him and Elaine in better days.

"Elaine and Travis. Forever," Angela read aloud from the back of the plastic photo. "Who is Elaine? She is beautiful."

"My wife," Travis replied quietly. He swallowed. "She is dead."

"Oh, I'm so sorry," Angela said. And then she asked the fateful question. "When did she die?"

It was a natural question. People always asked that. But it was something he wished he didn't have to reveal. Yet, he couldn't lie about it because that would have been unfair to Elaine. Like he was denying her very existence.

He was silent for so long that Angela looked up from the key ring. What was his problem? Why didn't he reply to her simple question.

"Travis?" she asked. There was something about the look on his face that caused a hard lump to form under her ribcage. What was wrong?

His jaw was set in a firm, hard line. "She died three weeks ago," he finally blurted out.

Three *weeks*?

"You mean three *years*," she said, hoping she'd heard wrong. Maybe three months?

Travis got up and reached for his clothes. Silently he got dressed and Angela's heart began to thump in heavy, ominous beats. It was obvious there was something he didn't want to say.

"What?" she asked.

"Three weeks," he at last said bluntly. "She died three weeks ago." It sounded to her like he was pushing the words out. Making sure she understood. "Just over three weeks actually."

Angela laid the key ring back on the dresser and walked to the door. "Goodbye, Travis," she said and quietly closed the door behind her.

In her cabin she stood for several minutes in the

middle of the room, confused. What had just happened? She walked to the window. Evening had fallen and the ocean was dark, unseen, except for the glimmer of the city lights that danced on the waves. The ship was due to leave shortly.

Her stomach growled, reminding her she hadn't had dinner yet, but the thought of food repelled her. Still, breakfast was far away and she really needed to eat something salty so she wouldn't start to feel queasy when the ship began to head for their last port of call.

She went to the dining room, hoping Travis hadn't had the same idea, because she didn't want to speak to him right now. Or even look at him. Not before she had sorted out her own thoughts about this whole affair. Affair! What an appropriate word! But all she knew was that Travis had been married, his wife had died three weeks ago, and he was now having sex.

He wasn't at their usual table but Angela feared he might show up, so instead she went to the cafe and ordered a simple grilled cheese sandwich. She forced herself to take bites from it and wash them down with gulps of coffee, while attempting to think through what had just happened. It was not pleasant.

The fact that Travis had lost a wife just three weeks ago and had jumped into bed with the first woman who made herself available, spoke miles about his character. All not good. He was not being unfaithful, since he wasn't married any more. But he was definitely disrespectful. Disrespectful to his poor wife's memory. Oh, God! And *she* was the woman he was having sex with! The thought that she had made herself available to him with such abandon made her cringe.

It was absolutely not like her to have sex with a man after such a short acquaintance. And yet, that's exactly what she had done. She'd had sex with a man she didn't know at all, and had done things she had never done before. It didn't help to tell herself he had seemed so trustworthy, because it was now obvious she hadn't known Travis at all.

She had always taken pride in her ability to discern peoples' characters just by looking into their eyes. Surely there must have been some signs that would have told her Travis was not what he seemed. Surely! If only she hadn't been so blinded by her attraction for him. But there was no excuse for her wanton behaviour. God, why had she trusted him, when there had really been nothing to go on, except a few days of friendship? What had he said or done to make her feel like she could open herself up to him? Nothing! She should have used her own discretion instead of letting Sylvia's words lure her into "letting her hair down".

Angela snorted. Sure, blame her best friend! It had nothing to do with Sylvia's words and everything to do

with her own lack of sound judgment. If she had followed her usual prudent behaviour, she would never
have jumped into bed with the first man who proposi-
tioned her on the trip.

That thought almost made her gag. She couldn't finish the sandwich and left to go out to pace the deck.
She took deep draughts of the cool night air and tried
to calm herself, but after only a few minutes the chilly
wind sent her back inside.

In her cabin she undressed, slipped under the cov-
ers, and tried to sleep. But her disobedient body refused to stop reminding her of the mind-blowing sex
she had just experienced with Travis. The cad. The
man with no scruples.

Head in his hands Travis sat slumped on the edge
of the bed that was still rumpled from their love-making. How come he hadn't said anything? Why hadn't
he done something to prevent her from leaving? He'd
stood there like an idiot and watched her close the
door in his face.

But perhaps it was for the best to end it now before
things got too hot. *Before* they got too hot? Damn!
Things already were too hot! He had just experienced
mind-numbing sex like he'd never had before.

He got up and began to pace the cabin, but after only
a few steps he found it too restricting and left to go out

on the deck. The chilly night breeze soon told him he should have worn a jacket but he stayed, marching briskly beside the railing, where the whoosh of the waves against the hull drowned out all other sounds. The ship had obviously left while they had been engaged in their sexual activities and hadn't even noticed.

On all his previous travels women had been out-of-bounds. So was that why, now that he was free, he had jumped into this intense relationship with Angela? Had he let himself go only because now he could? Or was there something more to this affair with Angela? He had to admit the intensity of his feelings for her was like nothing he'd ever experienced before. In fact, it was pretty close to blowing to smithereens his cynical ideas about love at first sight.

Travis shook his head. No, he couldn't allow this five-day fairy tale get him all mixed up and make him think it was something real. It wasn't. It was just an affair and only seemed special because it was the first love affair he'd ever experienced.

With Elaine it had been different. They'd been friends in high school and had begun dating after he went to art college in Calgary while she was studying physics in Calgary University. They'd been in love, but there had never been such intensity in their sex-life as tonight with Angela. They had always been best friends despite the total difference in their careers and their marriage had been good—while it lasted. Companionable and loving. Basically they knew everything about each other and could almost read each other's thoughts and finish each other's sentences.

The motion of the ship became more pronounced and Travis could see more whitecaps in the dark waters. A storm was approaching.

Travis snorted. Yeah, a storm all right, but not just on the ocean. Angela sure had brewed up a storm inside him as well.

But what did he know about her? Not much, except that her brother was an artist and she'd lived with her widowed mother for years. What did she do for a living? What were her interests? What kind of music did she like? She had said she had no boyfriend at the moment, but—though it didn't really matter—she must have had her share of lovers. She certainly seemed experienced, even though she claimed she'd never done some of the sex acts before. He found that hard to believe because she had been so free and easy in her love-making. So really, what did he actually know about her? It was lucky this affair had been nipped in the bud.

There was only one more day of sightseeing in the city of Palma, and if Angela went on the bus, he could very well go around Palma on his own. The following morning they would disembark in Barcelona and his flight for Calgary would leave in the early afternoon. He had no idea what Angela was going do after she got off the ship. Maybe she was going to take in Barcelona for a few days? That was fine. At least then they wouldn't board the same plane by accident.

A blast of cold wind sent a shiver through him and at last Travis had to give in and go back inside. As he walked along the corridors, he found himself having to take hold of the railings along the walls from time to time in order to maintain his balance. Yes, a storm was definitely brewing.

It was still early in the evening and he hadn't had anything to eat since lunch, but he wasn't hungry. In his cabin he snapped on the TV and threw himself onto his bed, but it was impossible to concentrate on the movie he'd chosen. The ship continued to rock but that didn't bother him. It was the memory of Angela's touch and their incredible sex that made him seethe in pain and frustration.

The next morning the continuing storm kept many passengers from the breakfast tables but after almost 24-hours of fasting and a sleepless night, Travis was ready for a fill-up. He couldn't help looking around the dining room for Angela. Maybe if he explained the situation surrounding Elaine's death to her, she would be willing to—

Forget that! A woman like Angela would never understand.

And, anyway, she was nowhere to be seen. Maybe the motion of the ship had got to her and she couldn't face food this morning. Or maybe the emotional storm of yesterday was the problem. Travis felt a stab of guilt for his part in it but didn't know how it could have been avoided. The facts surrounding Elaine were what they were and there was nothing he could do to change them.

At last the ship docked on the Island of Mallorca and ceased its erratic movements. Standing at the railing, Travis kept an eye on the people who were filing down the gangplank, eager to be on firm ground again, but Angela wasn't among them. Undecided as to what he should do, he finally joined the line-up and got on the bus. If Angela appeared, he could always . . . what? Slip out of the bus? Sit beside her as though it was game as usual? What?

But his worry was all for nothing, for she didn't come. Could the feeling inside him be classified as disappointment or relief? Strange. He couldn't decide.

The bus first took them to the Bellver Castle-fortress from the 13th century. When Travis crossed the moat into the stone courtyard, it was like entering medieval times. From the ramparts he had a great view of the Palma harbour and surroundings, but something was missing. Angela wasn't there to listen to his observations and provide her own comments. She wasn't there to give him feed-back by relating her thoughts to him. What would she have said about the intriguing round shape of the castle? Would she have made her little ohh and ahh sounds as she took in the magnificent view of the town?

Feeling forlorn, Travis got back on the bus which now took them to the monastery at Valldemossa where Frédéric Chopin, ill with tuberculosis, had lived for one miserable winter with his lover, George Sands, and her children. The rooms they had occupied had been made into a small museum and as Travis wandered through them, he became even more depressed. The guide had told them about the sad state of affairs between the lovers. It seemed that Sands' daughter, who was not happy with her mother's relationship with Chopin, had dressed up like a monk to frighten him. Chopin, thinking she was a ghost, had gone to the sacristan to ask for absolution. The priest had told him to stop having sex with Sands, and from that day on they had never slept together again.

This tale, whether true or not, was like a confirmation of how things were between him and Angela. Like Chopin and Sands, he and Angela would never have sex again. This dragged his mood down even more. But it wasn't just the thought of no sex that caused him such pain. It was the knowledge that he would never be able to talk with her, never hear her laugh, never share his thoughts and feelings with her. She was gone from his life.

He spent the last evening of the voyage in the lounge watching the show the crew put on for the passengers. Although he felt like moping in a corner by himself, he tried to put on a cheerful face for his table companions. He didn't know what he would have said to her if Angela had show up, but he needn't have worried. She stayed away.

On the last morning Angela choked down some toast and coffee and then returned to her cabin to collect her belongings. Her suitcase had already been taken and transported to the dock, where it was waiting for her to pick it up and put it into a cab. Then she would be off to the airport and home.

Queuing up to disembark, Angela stood and waited for the line to start moving. She smiled wanly when a fellow passenger asked her why she hadn't been to the reception with Travis the night before. Or on the trip to Palma with Travis the day before. Angela didn't want to feed the person's curiosity and simply blamed the storm for missing everything.

"I didn't feel well," she said. "The storm really got to me." There. That should take care of every question the woman might have in her mind. Except why Travis wasn't with her now.

Of course it wasn't the storm on the ocean that was the problem, but the storm in her heart. Her reluctance to come face to face with Travis had kept her from the main breakfast room. And last night she had called room service and ordered a small salad, which she had left mostly uneaten.

She was surprised at the deep disappointment that filled her so completely. There was no reason for her to feel this despondent. What kind of a hussy was she, to jump into bed with a man whom she had only met? Shame and embarrassment were what she should have been feeling instead of disappointment—instead of this great sadness that had taken over her heart.

She had to forget everything they had done together. Everything! But despite her angry self-chastisement, memory of the afternoon in Travis's cabin made the heat rise to her cheeks and her body respond in a totally forbidden way. Although the man had taken possession of her thoughts and captured her body, she *had* to forget him. Forget *everything*.

She sighed. Yes, it might be very difficult, if not impossible, to ever forget what had happened on this cruise, but she had to try to tuck him away, along with the photos and other mementoes of this trip. She could only hope that in time he would only come to her thoughts when something jogged her memory.

The line started to move.

"Angela."

Reluctantly she turned around to face Travis. "Good morning, Travis," she said as evenly and politely as possible, although she wished she could have just escaped into the crowd.

He took her by the arm. "Listen, could we talk?"

"I'm sorry. I don't want to lose my place in line," she said. Granted, it was a very weak excuse, but it was the best she could come up with on the spur of the moment. She wished he would just release her arm because it would look pretty silly if she tried to yank herself free.

But he didn't. "Please?" His grip tightened and he tried to lead her off to the side. "I want to tell you about—"

The people around them were looking at this exchange with interest.

"I really have to . . ." What excuse could she give? She could say she had ordered a taxi that was waiting for her, but the line of waiting taxis on the dock would very clearly show she was lying. In desperation she held out her hand to him. "Good-bye, Travis. It was very kind of you to keep me company during the cruise."

Relief washed over her as he released her arm, but

the relief was strangely mixed with regret.

With the line moving slowly toward the exit and the gangplank, and with all the curious eyes on them, there was little Travis could do but shake her hand. "Good-bye," he muttered gloomily and moved off to one side.

Angela turned away from him, gripped the handle of her overnight case and rolled it forward a few feet. Soon she disappeared into the crowd.

Travis was filled with a deep sense of loss. Would he ever see her again? Not likely, since his flight was leaving for Calgary in a few hours and hers—whenever she was flying home—would take her to Toronto. Separated by almost twenty-seven hundred kilometres, they were hardly going to be neighbours. But it might as well be the distance to the moon, because to Angela he was some immoral low-life she never wanted to see again.

Travis sighed, picked up his flight bag and went to the back of the line. What a way to finish what was supposed to be a relaxing holiday, following his work stint and the funeral before that. It was supposed to have helped him get a new grip on life and help him focus on something other than the nursing home. Yes, he'd found something to focus on, all right, but not what he'd expected. He truly hadn't thought he would get involved with any woman so soon after Elaine's death, although eventually finding someone new to share his life had definitely been at the back of his mind for some time. He was too young to spend the rest of his life a widower, and had hoped he would get married again. Maybe even start a family.

The speed with which he had taken to Angela surprised him. Especially going to bed with her. That was the most unexpected thing about this whole affair, because he never thought he was the kind of guy who would jump into bed with a woman he'd only met. But what had really thrown him for a loop was the intensity of the sex they had shared and the incredible pleasure it had brought to both of them. He knew she had enjoyed it as much as he. His body now reacted to the memory and he willed himself to think of something else.

Angela. What else was there to think about?

Travis moved forward a few feet. Now that the cruise was irrevocably over, everyone was keen to get off the ship and stood toe-to-heel, as though that would get them off the ship any faster. Most of the people were probably looking forward to flying home after their summer adventures.

Not Travis. What was waiting for him at home? His days and his thoughts had been filled with Elaine for so long that it would be difficult to start focusing on something new. He had thought about maybe taking up painting again. It would be interesting to see if he still had what it took. Maybe he could start by painting some of the great landscapes and gardens he'd photographed on this trip. Or maybe a portrait of Angela as she'd been on the bed, her hair tousled and her lips parted and glowing from his kisses.

Stop right there! That memory brought such a feeling of desire, but at the same time of loss, that he had to tell himself sternly to think about something else. He must not think about her! But still he couldn't help craning his neck to see over the heads of his fellow passengers. There she was, hurrying toward a waiting row of taxis. She opened the back door of the cab at the front of the line and slipped in. The driver lifted her suitcase into the trunk, slammed the back door shut to hide her from view, and pulled off into the traffic.

Angela was gone.

Chapter Five

"Welcome home, Angela!"

Sylvia's hug at the Arrivals felt incredibly comforting after the eight-hour flight during which Angela had barely eaten, hadn't watched a single movie, or even opened her book. She was angry with herself for feeling so depressed, but somehow she couldn't seem to shake this morose feeling. How could one man make her feel this low? She'd broken up with men before but never had such an ache filled her heart as now.

"Wow, the flight sure took its toll on you," Sylvia said. "You look awfully tired and drawn. Even your usually smooth and bronzed colour is off."

Sylvia, on the other hand, Angela observed, was a picture of health as always. Her long, blond hair was pulled back into a pony-tail and her strong arms, chiseled into shape at the gym, now released Angela from the welcoming embrace.

"I would have though the Spanish sunshine would

have given you a lovely tan and instead you look pale as ashes," Sylvia continued as she grabbed the handle of Angela's suitcase.

Angela was too tired to put up a polite argument. Besides, she know her friend was quite capable of pulling the heavy luggage over the uneven pavement of the parking lot.

"I felt I was coming down with something just before boarding. And not being able to sleep on the flight didn't help." It was surprising how easily the little white lie slipped out. Not something Angela normally engaged in, but she didn't want to start unloading her troubles on her friend the minute they met. Even though Sylvia was her bestie from high school days she wasn't planning to say anything about what had happened between her and Travis. It would have started a conversation that she didn't even want to think about.

"I assume you want me to drive you to your condo?" Sylvia asked, as she put her car in reverse. "Although I know you're anxious to see how the twins have grown in the time you've been away."

Angela laughed. "Probably they're already reading, smart little fellows as they are. But, yes, I want to go home first. I'll unpack, take a shower and freshen up before driving over to the house. I brought a few little gifts for everyone. I want to see how Alexander and

André like their stuffed toy bulls."

"Bulls?"

"Of course. I was in Spain, remember?"

"Did you meet any cute Spaniards? I'm dying to see your pictures. Especially the ones of the tall, dark and handsome men you met."

Sylvia was getting onto the expressway, and had to be mindful as she joined the rush hour traffic, so she was too busy to notice the flush that rose onto Angela's cheeks.

"Oh, there were dozens of those, for sure," Angela threw out as casually as she could and laughed to cover up the turmoil inside her. "It was hard to decide who was the tallest and darkest and handsomest."

"Hah! In just one week you couldn't have been *that* busy, you little liar," Sylvia exclaimed. "Even though you have your Spanish good looks."

Angela decided to reveal just a bit of the truth. After all, Sylvia would ask about Travis in the photo taken at Gibraltar, so it was probably better to mention it now, and make it sound like it was just something casual. "All right," she said. "Would you settle for one tall, not dark, but handsome man?"

"Sounds good to me."

Sylvia parked her car in the visitor parking in front of Angela's condo and then helped with the suitcase again as they took the elevator up to the 19th floor.

"Well, I'll leave you to get yourself tidied up," Sylvia said. "But Jeff and I would like for you to come for dinner on Friday. We both want to get the lowdown on your trip. And see pictures of this tall, not dark, but handsome specimen."

"Thanks. That would be great," Angela said. Her stomach was starting to remind her she hadn't eaten since she left Spain. "And thank you so much for picking me up at the airport."

"Any time, my dear," Sylvia gave Angela another hug. "Maybe the twins will cheer you up and make you look less like a lost ghost."

Now that she was safely on her own familiar territory where her friends and family were, Angela was sure she would soon start to get a grip on herself and feel more like her old, cheerful self.

Travis was now safely out of her life for good.

Angela drove up the long driveway of the house she'd called home all her life. She loved the three-storey brownstone, over a hundred years old, which her grandparents had bought after immigrating from Spain in the 1920s. The house held such a wealth of memories, for not only had Angela's mother, an only child, been born there, but so had Angela and Miguel. The huge trees shading the house, like guardians of the family history, were as old as the building itself, and were kept meticulously pruned. And Angela knew her mother's gardens outside the solarium would be blooming with a glorious display of colours.

She stepped into the familiar foyer, filled with the delicious aroma of cooking. The pandemonium that her arrival created dispelled any remaining thoughts of Travis. Miguel and Marita rushed up to welcome her with warm hugs and exclamations of welcome. The twins crawled on the floor between everyone's legs, making delighted sounds at seeing their Aunty Angela again. Each boy wanted his share of her attention.

Angela picked one of them up. "Alexander! Wait till you see what Auntie Angela brought you from Spain!" she cooed. She placed Alexander down on the floor and picked up the brother. "André, you're not supposed to be pushing your brother, you little imp." And as Alexander put up a howl, grabbing her legs, she laughed. "I can't hold you both in my arms at the same time any more. You're getting too big."

When the twins had been thoroughly kissed and greeted, Miguel took her into his arms again and hugged her tightly. More tightly than was customary between them, Angela noted with surprise. It wasn't like her brother could have missed her *that* much. She searched his face for an explanation and her heart sank. There was sadness in his dark eyes.

"What is it, Miguel?" she asked, dreading his answer.

"Is it Mother?"

He nodded. "Yes." He led her off to the library for privacy and closed the door behind them. "She's not well. That's why she's not here to greet you. She's waiting for you in the solarium."

"What happened?" Angela whispered. Her voice refused to co-operate.

"It's her heart," Miguel said. "She had a massive heart attack just after you left."

"Miguel, why didn't you let me know?" Angela cried angrily. "I would have come home!"

"Mother wouldn't hear of it," Miguel said. "She absolutely did *not* allow us to let you know. You know how she is. She wanted you to have a good time on the cruise and not worry about her. She said you would just waste your time sitting by her hospital bed. She is home now because she wanted to come home to . . ." Miguel swallowed. "To die."

He held her arm as Angela, on rubbery legs, walked beside him down the hall. In the solarium Mrs. Cordova was lying on the day bed, covered with a light quilt. A nurse was sitting nearby, holding a magazine that she had obviously been reading to the patient. As Miguel and Angela entered, the nurse rose and greeted them with a smile before moving off to sit by the window.

Angela noted that her mother's hair was carefully

coiffed, as always, but was now showing the gray that was usually hidden by a rinse. Mrs. Cordova held out a trembling hand and Angela rushed to her side.

"Mother! How are you?" Angela knelt by the day bed, grasping the fragile hand in both of hers. "Miguel told me you're not well." Her mother had always reminded Angela of a little sparrow, but now as Angela gave her a hug, she could feel almost every brittle bone of the thin body under her hands. Afraid of hugging her too tightly, Angela instead stroked the shrunken cheek.

"Yes, I don't believe I am too well," Mrs. Cordova conceded with a slight smile. It was probably meant to comfort her daughter, but instead caused tears to well into Angela's eyes.

"Miguel didn't let me know about your illness. I would have come home."

"To do what?" her mother snapped. Though her voice was hardly more than a whisper, it still showed her old spirit. "It was my decision not to interrupt your holiday. I trust you had a good time?"

"Yes, Mother, I did," Angela replied and immediately saw doubt flash in her mother's sharp brown eyes. Obviously her response wasn't convincing enough.

"What happened?" Though still weak, the voice had some of its old commanding tone and Angela had to smile through her tears.

"Nothing happened," she said, hoping to appease her

mother. "I had a great time."

Mrs. Cordova frowned. "Something happened. I *thought* you didn't look very well when you walked in just now."

"Mother!" Angela cried. "I've just had an eight-hour flight and didn't sleep a wink. Of course I look awful."

"I am not dead yet," her mother whispered, more weakly now. She was obviously loosing strength. "Please don't try to fool me."

Angela looked up at Miguel for help. He shook his head. "I think we better let you rest, Mother," he said as Angela got to her feet. "Too much excitement isn't good for you."

"Yes, too much excitement isn't good for me,'" Mrs. Cordova mimicked in a whisper, puckering up her face. "Such a clichéd expression. I wish you wouldn't use it, Miguel."

Miguel smiled and bent down to give his mother a kiss on the forehead. "Sorry, Mother, I won't use it again. Angela, remember not to tell Mother she's had too much excitement."

Angela kissed Mrs. Cordova's withered cheek and walked out with Miguel. Fear of impending death filled her and she turned once more to look at her mother through the glass doors of the solarium. The nurse had risen and had taken out the blood pressure monitor.

Angela paced her condo, walking from one room to the next and back again. Her slippers shuffled softly on the shiny wooden floors and her red velvet robe trailed behind her like a matador's cape. In frustration she ran her fingers through her hair which she hadn't yet put up in the customary bun. It was already late in the afternoon and she had yet to get dressed.

What should she do?

It was only a few weeks since Mother had been laid to rest beside her husband and her in-laws in the family vault. The will had been read, and Angela now had a sizeable inheritance to deal with. All this money, and she didn't know how to best utilize it. The frustrating thing was, she wanted to make sure she did the right thing and didn't squander it away, but she had no idea what she should do. Like a high school kid pondering a future career, here she was, at almost forty, trying to decide what she should do with the rest of her life.

The purpose of the trip had been to plan her future as an independent woman. She hadn't known, of course, that she would soon be a *rich* independent woman. This fact opened up more doors for her. Too many confusing doors. And the trip had definitely not been helpful. It had, in the end, confused her even more and had given her this empty feeling in her heart that refused to go away.

She stopped in front of the hall mirror and stared at

the dark hair flowing over her shoulders. Travis. He had asked her to let down her hair and in a haze she had complied. She had let her hair down all the way, and what had that led to? It still made her blush just thinking of what she and Travis had done. What *she* had done. And what she had to show for it was embarrassment and a huge disappointment not only in herself, but in the man who had let her down. He had turned out to be an unfeeling cad.

She had always been responsible and restrained as far as men were concerned. It had been her *modus operandi* in life. No foolish side-steps or crazy, dangerous adventures. She wasn't like that in anything. Her few sexual encounters had been level-headed, and she had gone into them with her eyes wide open.

So what had happened on the cruise? What she had done had been totally out of character! She still couldn't understand how she could have let herself fall into that deep well head first. How stupid she had been. How incautious.

She marched into the bedroom. Angrily she grabbed a fistful of hair and pushed it up. Never again would she be caught with her hair down. She picked up a bunch of pins and stabbed them into her hair. There!

It was now several weeks since the cruise, but she still hadn't been able to forget Travis. Even though, since coming home, thoughts of him had taken a back seat to the worry over her mother. Angela had spent all her time at her old home with her mother and then, when she died, making funeral arrangements, and dealing with lawyers. It was only at night, when her mind was free to play devious tricks on her, that Travis still visited her. How she resented these dreams. She was angry with herself for having succumbed to his charms and allowing herself to be so free in her love-making with him. So wanton.

Or perhaps she simply regretted that the relationship that had started out with such promise, had gone so horribly wrong.

It was time to get dressed. She was due to be at Sylvia and Jeff's in an hour. Because of everything that had happened since her return, the promised dinner had had to wait till now and she was looking forward to getting her friend's thoughts on what she should do. Not to mention some very sincere tea and sympathy.

Sylvia and Jeff welcomed her warmly into their modern home, so different from the Cordova house where everything was influenced by old, heavy Spanish decor. Angela and Sylvia had been best friends since high school and Jeff had just naturally joined them when he and Sylvia had started dating.

Angela hoped she would not stutter and stammer when she had to mention Travis to her friends. She hoped he no longer would affect her. At least not much. But as soon as she began to show the photos after dinner, she felt less in charge of her emotions. She willed her voice not to give her away as she knew the picture of Travis at Gibraltar was coming up. She had already deleted the pictures of their kiss because that surely would have produced a veritable thunderstorm! Now she took a sip of her tea to fortify herself.

"My, oh, my!" Sylvia breathed as she inspected the picture of Travis with the monkey. "So, one of these is the tall, not dark, but handsome man you mentioned?"

Angela burst out laughing. "Yes. Guess which one."

"Hmm." Sylvia brushed her chin with her thumb. "Let me see . . ."

"I think I know," Jeff put in. "Is he the one with hair only on his head? The other guy's kind of hairy all over."

"Good boy! You got it, Jeff!" Angela tried to keep her voice light and playful to hide the emotions the smiling face in the photo stirred in her.

"My, but he *is* gorgeous," Sylvia exclaimed.

"Yes, the monkey sure is cute, isn't he?" Angela said. A confusing mixture of longing, anger and sadness filled her and she forced herself to remain jovial.

"I think Sylvia is talking about the man," Jeff put in. "Aren't you, dear?"

Sylvia continued to examine Travis closely. "Yes, I am. I certainly am. I assume you traded emails and phone numbers and other vital info with him?" She sighed deeply. "Now why didn't *I* go along with you on this fateful voyage?"

Fateful! What an accurate word her friend had unknowingly used.

"Because you have your gym business to take care of," Angela reminded her. "Besides, Jeff would have wanted to come along and that would have limited your flirting with the gorgeous guys," she added, laughing.

"Too true," Sylvia said with mock dismay and then went on, brightening up. "So what's the name of this Gorgeous George and where does he live?"

"His name is Travis Jordan and he lives in Calgary. Much too far for any relationships. So we ended it before it even began."

"Now that was pretty silly of you," Sylvia cried. "Have you not heard of airplanes? A few thousand kilometres by air is like a few hundred clicks by car."

"I know, but carrying on a relationship would have been too complicated." Of course she had walked out of his cabin before that subject had even come up. And probably it never would have, since he seemed to be the kind of man who would jump into bed with the first available woman. Before or after his wife's death—it probably didn't matter. "Luckily we never reached the stage where staying connected was even discussed,"

Angela continued. "Besides, maybe he already had a girlfriend." She hoped that would get Sylvia off the trail.

"Well, I still say you should have taken down his email address at the very least so you could have exchanged photos with him. Never know where that may have led," Sylvia declared. "Now please excuse me while I drool over him."

With mock annoyance Jeff grabbed the phone from her. "Enough drooling, little wife."

"Oh, but the monkey is such a cute fellow!" Sylvia cried, trying to grab the phone back from her husband.

Angela forced a giggle. "The monkey is the reason I took the pic. Travis just thrust himself in."

Sylvia got up to gather the tea cups and take them to the sink. "Yeah, right. But were there really no sparks at all between you two?"

"None." Angela had to cross her fingers behind her back as she pronounced the word with conviction. She would never reveal the truth about the sparks that had flown between them when Travis had held her on the dance floor. Nor about the fireworks when they were in bed. Even thinking about all that was like scratching at a bleeding wound she was trying so desperately to heal.

Sylvia returned to the living room with a wine bottle and stemmed glasses. She poured each of them a drink and sat down beside Angela on the couch. "So did you come up with any thoughts or ideas while on the cruise as far as a new career is concerned?"

Angela laughed. "A *new* career? You mean as opposed to an *old* career?"

"Wrong choice of words. Just career, then."

"Nope. Nothing at all." Angela leaned back onto the cushions in a show of defeat. "My brain is in a fog. I can't get a single clear thought to pierce through the mist."

"Don't be so hard on yourself," Jeff comforted her. "You've gone through a lot and this will all take time for you to work out."

"Thank you. But I really want to get doing something. I'm not getting any younger, you know. I've been thinking that I probably will have to go back to school. But at my age that doesn't sound very inviting."

"Well, if you start our own business, it would be very useful to take a business course," Sylvia put in.

Angela looked at her friend with one raised eyebrow. "Exactly what business am I starting?" she asked.

But Sylvia didn't look daunted. "I've been thinking about those lovely things you've designed and knit for your friends. I get so many compliments on the sweater you gave me a couple of years ago. You could open a shop and sell them." She picked up her wine glass and took a sip. "Eh?"

Angela shook her head. "I could never knit enough to make a living. My designs are so complicated they're very slow to knit."

"Hmm, you're probably right," Sylvia mused. Then she brightened up. "How about something to do with flowers? You took care of the plants in your mother's solarium for years so you know flowers. And you have an artistic eye, so taking a course in flower designing might be just up your alley. You could open a florist shop."

Angela took a sip of her wine. "Well . . . that sounds like a possibility," she agreed. "But to be a florist, besides taking a flower design course, I'd probably have to take some kind of a course to learn about the many different kinds of plants and how to care for them. Plus take a business course so I could learn how to take care of the books and orders and bills and all that. That's a lot of courses! Maybe the wool shop would be a better choice."

"Yes!" Sylvia enthused. "And you already know a lot about different wools and where you can get them. You've ordered them for years."

Angela smiled at her friend's excitement. "Yes, that's true."

Sylvia grinned. "So now that you've made up your mind—"

"I have done no such thing," Angela said laughing.

"But I *will* look into both the flower shop and the wool shop ideas."

"And also look into a business course," Jeff helpfully reminded her.

Chapter Six

A few weeks later Angela hesitantly entered a classroom at the Georgian Community College, where she had signed up for a six-month evening course on managing a small business. To her relief many of the fifteen people in the room appeared to be well into their thirties, or even forties. Most were women, but there were also a few men sitting at the long tables, waiting for the teacher to arrive. And there wasn't a single teenager in sight, thank goodness.

Angela sat beside a man who gave her a welcoming smile. He was blond and looked to be in his early forties. She smiled back at him and set her binder on the table in front of her.

"So, you're planning to start a business?" the man asked, starting the conversation. "Or is that a redundant question?"

"Well, I'm thinking of it," Angela replied, fingering her binder. "I'm not sure yet. I'm hoping this course will let me know if I'm the kind of person who can make a business succeed."

"I suppose it depends a lot on the type of business," the man said. "But you may be right. Some people may not be cut out to run *any* business." He held out his hand which looked strong, tanned and somewhat calloused. "My name is Steve Jamieson." His smile was open and friendly and immediately made Angela feel at ease.

"Angela Cordova." It felt nice to have her hand enclosed by his large one in a friendly grip.

"Sounds Spanish," Steve observed.

"It is."

At that point the teacher entered the room and got the class started, putting an end to any further chatting. The woman seemed very efficient and knowledgeable and she brought out many salient points in her presentation. Angela took copious notes and listened with great interest.

By the time the teacher called a coffee break, Angela knew this course was just what she needed.

"Were you going to go to the cafeteria to have a coffee or something?" Steve asked, getting up. He bent backwards, hands on his haunches, and had a small stretch. "I was going to walk down for a bit of exercise and pick up a chocolate bar."

"Yes. I think I'll come down, too," Angela replied,

getting out of her seat. "Sitting in one spot, paying close attention and taking notes for an hour and a half makes me feel I could use a cup of tea."

They walked downstairs together and sat at one of the small round tables, where Angela sipped her hot drink and Steve crunched his candy bar.

"I'm a chocolate addict," Steve confessed with a smile. Angela very much liked his friendly demeanor.

"I think most of us are," she said with a laugh. "I just try not to indulge myself."

They walked back to class, and the lesson continued, with Angela filling up page after page of notes. She expected this information would prove useful when she started her business. By the end of the evening Angela felt very satisfied with what she had learned so far.

She walked to her car in the inadequately lit dark parking lot and to her surprise she found Steve following her. What was the man doing? Did he think she was in need of a body guard? She hoped he didn't have something sinister in mind. She dug out her keys and pressed the unlock button.

"Looks like we parked almost side by side. Mine's this blue Ford," Steve said. "I'll see you next week." With a small wave he got into his car and drove off.

Angela chuckled to herself. How silly of her to imagine Steve could be a sex-offender or something worse.

He was just another student, out to learn about starting a business, just as she was. She started the motor
and drove home, happy with her first evening.

The following week she again sat beside Steve and it
was natural to walk to the cafeteria with him during
the break. They chatted about the course, and Angela
was surprised how much they had to talk about. Steve
was serious about the painting company he was planning to start. Angela followed his lead and told him
about her own business plans, and so their conversa-
tions never strayed into anything personal.

Having conferred with Sylvia and her brother, she
had finally made her decision. She would open up a
small wool boutique where she would sell not only
yearns, but also her own designs. She planned to hire
a few people to do most of the knitting as piecework
for the shop. And if a customer wanted to have a
sweater done on order, she could have that item done
by one of the knitters, or she could do it herself. She
had yet to find a location for her shop, but felt confident she would eventually find something suitable.

A few weeks later, Angela and Steve once again stood
beside their cars after the class, talking animatedly
about the evening's lessons. Since the first night they
had continued to park close to the same spots, and so

always ended up walking to their vehicles together. Tonight a bitter wind blew from the north signaling the approach of winter. It whirled fallen leaves around the parking lot along with paper coffee cups and other discarded debris.

Angela pulled her coat tightly around her. "I guess there's no denying it. Winter is just around the corner. I'm afraid I can't stand here talking tonight because I'm already freezing. Obviously I should have worn a heavier coat."

"I hate to miss our after-class chat," Steve said ruefully. "Could we go back in and get something warm to drink at the cafeteria? That way we could continue our talk?"

Angela didn't hesitate. "Yes, That is a good idea. Let's do that." She was happy to continue what had already become a tradition.

In the cafeteria she noted that with the location change, so did their topic of conversation. It became more personal.

"So, where do you work?" Steve asked after they'd settled down with their hot chocolates.

"Actually, I don't work anywhere." How strange it sounded to say that. As though she were some rich heiress who just lived off her inheritance. To mitigate her leisure-sounding life-style she added, "But when I open up my wool shop I expect to be working long hours."

"Yes, owning a business is like that," Steve said. "I also expect to be working long hours with my painting business. I just don't know if I'll have the funds to get all the stuff I'll need to get it up and running."

"Such as. . . ?"

"A truck or a van will be the most expensive item. Then all the ladders, brushes, cleaners, drop cloths and such."

Thinking about her own carefree financial situation, Angela felt sorry for him. "But didn't you tell me before you're working for a painting company?"

"Sure, but the pay's terrible."

"But surely you'll be able to get a loan from your bank?"

Steve dropped his gaze and fidgeted with his serviette. "Normally, yes, but I'm having bit of a problem with my credit rating."

He looked up at her and on his face Angela could see embarrassment. It made her very uncomfortable to talk about his finances, and she was reluctant to continue the conversation. What he had done to wreck his credit rating was no business of hers.

But Steve seemed ready to expose his past without her encouragement. "It was my wife." He shook his head to indicate the woman was trouble. "When we divorced she pretty well took me to the cleaners. The bank repossessed my car when I couldn't make the payments, and now that prevents me from getting a loan for another vehicle."

Despite her decision not to probe into his affairs, she had to make a comment. "But the car you're driving—"

"It's my sister's. She loans it to me on course nights so I can come here."

"Oh."

Steve cheered up and grinned. "But hey, that's not your worry. I'll be good once my painting business is going and I get some clients." He laughed ruefully. "I don't suppose you need a room painted?"

"I am afraid not." Angela almost wished she did. "But I can ask around and see if anyone does." Why was she saying these things? Why was she getting involved? What she was hearing sounded so sad but she didn't want to continue talking about this. Here he was, taking this course just like she was, both of them hoping to become proficient at handling their business affairs, but he didn't have the money to even get started. She had to hand it to him, he certainly was an optimist.

"I . . . I hope things work out for you," she stammered. She was embarrassed by her pitifully weak response, but what else could she say? She wasn't going to loan him the necessary money even though it was within her power to do so. After all, what did she know about him? Nothing at all. Aside from the weekly chats at coffee breaks and after class, he was almost a total stranger. Hardly what one would call a best friend. Not even a friend, really. A casual acquaintance was more like it. A classmate.

Steve reached across the table to grasp her hand. "I know they will." His voice was comforting, as though *she* was the one with the money worries.

His hazel eyes, looking into hers, were honest and frank. She had always taken pride in her ability to read people's eyes and she liked his.

She started. But what about on the ship! God! How could her skills have failed her so completely in that situation? She could have wagered her soul that Travis was a great guy, but somehow she had failed to see any warning signs in his eyes of the callous shallowness lurking inside him. Not even when they had been in his cabin and had—

She pulled her hand away. "Hey, it's getting late!" she cried, glancing at her watch. "I better get going home."

"What's your hurry? It's only just after ten." Steve again tried to take her hand but she avoided it by reaching for her purse on the seat beside her.

"I have an early appointment tomorrow morning," she said and immediately her face flushed hot. Had she really resorted to a lie in order to extricate herself from this situation? This was terrible! Here she had just been remembering how deceitful Travis had been, and now it was obvious that in a pinch she wasn't above being just as mendacious. She had no right to judge anybody.

The next few weeks sped by as Angela began to seriously look for a location for her wool shop.

"Your knits are so fabulous, and also so expensive, that I think the shop should be in a location where rich people will come to buy," Sylvia opined. "Maybe a boutique in some ritzy downtown shopping mall."

They were sitting at Angela's kitchen table, shifting through rent ads for business. Between them sat a bottle of fine Spanish red.

Angela thanked her lucky stars she didn't have to worry about the up-front costs of opening such a shop. "I think you are right. But what do you think of the name I've picked out for it—'Woolly Bear Yarns and Knits'? My logo will be a cute woolly bear caterpillar."

"I think that's sweet," Sylvia enthused. "Since you're going to sell wool as well as your knits and patterns, it's perfect! Let's drink to 'Woolly Bear Yarns and Knits'!" She raised her glass and took a sip. "It's good you're taking that business course, because without it your head would be a mixed-up mess with all the details you're having to go through."

"I'm still looking for knitters who are talented enough to follow my complicated patters," Angela said. "I'd like to have a few sweaters ready to showcase when I open. I have a shipment of fine wools coming from England, but until I get a shop, I'll have to store them in the house. Miguel and Marita are so supportive of my project."

Then, out of the blue, Sylvia asked, "How are things with Steve? Are you getting any more romantic with him?"

"Oh, goodness, no! Not at all," Angela exclaimed with a laugh, but then added, "Although lately Steve *has* intimated he'd like to be more of a boyfriend than just a friend. But I really don't feel anything special for him. He even tried to give me a lovely silk scarf as a gift, but I refused to accept it."

"That's too bad. No sparks at all then?"

"None, I'm afraid."

Sylvia frowned. "I'm worried about you. It looks like no man is able to get any sparks out of you. Even that gorgeous fellow on the cruise ship couldn't light you up. What's his name? Trevor something?"

How was Sylvia so cleverly able to throw a curve ball like that and mess up the day? Angela swallowed and took a deep breath before she was able to reply in a carefree tone. "Travis. His name is Travis Jordan." She turned her head and lowered her gaze to look at the ads. "And I don't think there's anything wrong with me just because neither he nor Steve happen to turn me on." She flipped a page over. "I'm just looking for something different."

"Something other than good looks? That's understandable. And Steve should fit that bill quite nicely. He's not exactly a Hollywood leading man type."

"Sylvia, that's not nice," Angela riposted. "He's a perfectly nice-looking man. Have you seen him smile?"

"Except in that photo you showed me, I haven't seen him, period."

Angela had pointed Steve out to Sylvia in a class photo that someone had taken and had distributed to everyone by e-mail.

"But I'll take your word for it. Yes, he's a perfectly nice-looking man." Sylvia shook her head. "But he's no match for that Travis."

Angela raised her chin defensively. "There are qualities in a man that are more important than good looks."

"Such as?"

"A sense of humour. Ability to communicate." She stopped and swallowed again, hoping her voice wouldn't catch at the next words. "And honesty. That's *really* important." Her voice slid into a whisper as she finished the sentence, and hoped Sylvia wouldn't read anything into that. She was relieved when her friend didn't seem to have noticed.

"I can't say I disagree with you," Sylvia said. "But which of those qualities did this Travis lack?"

Angela felt her face heat up as her heart suddenly sped up its tempo. She stood and turned to pour more wine into their glasses. Then she screwed the cap on with extra care before replying. "He couldn't seem to communicate," she finally forced out. Here she was again, covering up the truth. God! She was turning into an inveterate liar.

But was she? Pensively she took a sip from her glass. In a way, wasn't it his lack of communication about Elaine that had caused the problem between them? So she wasn't lying. Then she shook her head. No. Communication hadn't been the problem. It was deceit. He had known if he revealed that Elaine had just died, the end result would have been that they would never have made love. He had known it, and so had deceitfully said nothing in order to get her to bed with him.

"Yes," she pronounced, nodding decidedly, causing her friend to look up at her with a frown.

"Yes, what?" Sylvia asked. "And what was all that head-shaking and nodding about?"

Again Angela felt herself blushing. "Nothing. I mean, I was just thinking about something. It is not important."

"Okay, if you say so. But Steve can communicate, right?" Sylvia pursued. "I mean the poor guy doesn't create sparks, and yet he can—"

"Oh, for goodness sake. You and your sparks. It just so happens that yes, Steve *can* communicate. We always have a lot to talk about when we're together. We're both in the process of starting businesses and we compare notes. I'd say we're kind of like business friends."

"At least on your side. Right? You said he would like to be more than just a business friend."

"Yes. But that is not going to happen. And he knows it and he is all right with it. We still like to chat during the breaks and after class."

"All right, then," Sylvia said, but looked doubtful. "But I still don't see why—"

"Enough about men, Sylvia," Angela snapped. "We were talking about my business, remember? A much more relevant topic."

As winter approached and the weather got chillier, Angela and Steve no longer stopped on the parking lot to chat, but made their way to the cafeteria directly after class. This was the last evening of lessons and only one more class remained. It consisted of an exam for which Angela had been studying conscientiously.

"What are you doing for Christmas?" Steve asked out of the blue as they walked down the corridor to the cafeteria.

The question caught her by surprise. "I'll be going home to—" Suddenly it hit her that this would be the first Christmas without her mother and her eyes misted. "To my brother's," she finished and brushed away a tear with the back of her hand.

Steve's frowned. "What's the matter?" His voice reflected warmth and concern.

"I . . . I forgot for a moment. My mother is no longer there."

"She passed away recently?"

"Last summer."

"I'm so sorry." Steve reached out and placed an arm across her shoulder. The touch felt comforting and she didn't pull away.

"Thank you." She had a sudden urge to lean her head against his shoulder but quickly put the thought out of her mind. That would have given him the wrong signal.

They entered the cafeteria and after they had sat down at their customary table with their mugs of hot chocolate, he picked up the conversation. "So you're going to spend Christmas with your brother. Who else will be there?"

"His wife and their twin boys. We don't have a large

family, because when my grandparents immigrated from Spain, they left all their relatives behind. My father was their only child and he and my mother had only my bother and me." She smiled. "My little nephews—the twins—are so cute."

"You're lucky to have a close family, even if it's small." He sounded wistful. Perhaps even envious.

"You have your sister," Angela said. "Has she no children?"

"My sister?" Steve lowered his gaze. "No, unfortunately she doesn't."

"And you and your ex-wife didn't have any kids either?" It was almost strange that in all these months they had never spoken about their families.

He gave his hot chocolate a swirl with the wooden stir stick. "No," he at last replied.

"Oh." She knew this was her cue to ask this lonely man to come to her brother's home for Christmas dinner, but deep down she had no desire to bring Steve and his sister into their traditional Christmas celebration. This thought made her feel totally uncharitable. But, on the other hand, what did she know about Steve and his sister? They probably wouldn't like Spanish food or the Cordova customs. Angela shifted uncomfortably. Perhaps she should ask Miguel and Marita what they thought.

But Steve obviously wasn't harbouring any thoughts

of being invited. "Would you like to join me for dinner one evening?" he asked. "We could celebrate the end of the course."

Angela hesitated. Was there any harm in going for dinner with him? They had, after all, shared many mugs of hot chocolate. What was the difference if they had a bit more to eat?

"Yes, I think it would be nice to go to a restaurant with you. As you say, it will be chance to celebrate the end of the course and. . ." She didn't want to say it, but it would more than likely also be their farewell dinner.

"Great. Do you like Italian food? Greek? Thai? I'm afraid I don't know any Spanish restaurants."

"That is all right. Italian will be good," Angela replied. "If you give me your e-mail address I will let you know where we can meet."

As she was getting ready to go out for dinner with Steve, Angela passed her dresser on her way to the bathroom. She happened to look down at her car keys that lay there. What? "Elaine and Travis. Forever". Quickly she shut her eyes and when she opened them, the key fob again sported the familiar CAA tag. Annoyed with herself, Angela shook her head, marched into the bathroom and closed the door firmly after her. Such silliness!

She brushed her teeth, angrily spitting out the toothpaste as though that would remove any memories of Travis that persisted on invading her thoughts at the most inopportune times. Like now, when she was getting ready to go on a date. Enough time had passed since the cruise, so surely all thoughts of him should begin to recede by now. But too often he still came at night to tease her with his dimpled smile and his brown eyes that sparkled with humour. And in her dreams he still made her gasp and writhe under his ardent lovemaking. On those occasions she awoke, her hair damp and tangled and the bed sheets awry.

But it wasn't like she wanted to substitute that with dreams of Steve. Gosh, no! There was nothing sexual about her relationship with the man, thank goodness. They were only friends. And she definitely wasn't ready to jump into anything that would even remotely remind her of what she'd had with Travis.

Maybe she never would.

Angela chose a top and then looked at herself in the mirror. She removed the blouse, tossed it on a chair and went back into the walk-in closet to pick out another one. Why was she being so choosy when it was just Steve she was going out with? He was not someone special and close to her heart and it wasn't like she planned to see him again after the course was over. They were just going out for a celebratory dinner.

End of story.

Was she was being incautious, going out with a man she didn't know much about. Because what did she know about Steve besides the fact that he was divorced with no children, and that he had a kind sister who loaned him her car on course nights? Nothing.

But what had she known about Travis? Not even that much, and yet she had gone totally overboard with him.

Angela snorted. It wasn't like every man she would ever meet was going to be another Travis. She really had to stop being so distrustful.

Finally Angela chose a soft cashmere sweater that was nice and warm and only slightly sexy. A little bit of glamour wouldn't hurt. She slipped on earrings that dangled and—she was fully aware—showed off her long, graceful neck.

As she drove to the Italian restaurant she had an odd sense of betrayal. Which was totally silly. Whom was she betraying by having dinner with Steve? Absolutely no one. She tried to brush the feeling away by singing along with the Christmas song that was playing on the car radio. ". . . blue, blue Christmas without you!" Angela snapped off the sound and grimaced. Thank you, Elvis, for sounding so cheerful! Just the kind of uplifting song she needed to hear.

She entered the restaurant and immediately spotted

Steve, who got up and came to greet her. He was sporting a nice navy suit, very different from the casual clothes in which she always saw him at the college. Maybe she should have worn something more dressy, since he was so elegantly decked out, but she really hadn't considered this a real, honest-to-goodness date. It was only a dinner to celebrate the end of the course.

He smiled his wide smile. "Angela, it's great to see you. You look absolutely gorgeous."

When the waiter came to their table, she ordered a glass of wine to toast the occasion. She touched Steve's beer glass. "Here's to successful exams," she said and then added, "And to the end of our chats." That was, after all, the natural consequence of all this.

"Oh, no," Steve groaned. "Please don't say that. I want to see more of you, not less."

But that wasn't what she had in mind. "I don't think there's any reason for us to continue—"

"But there is!" he cried in earnest. "I have really looked forward to seeing you each week in class, and to not see you again would be . . . it would be disastrous."

Angela laughed. "An over-blown statement, Steve. There is nothing disastrous about us not seeing each other." As she said it, she meant it. Not seeing Steve ever again didn't stir up any angst inside her. "But it has been nice to have someone with whom I could share ideas and thoughts about the course." She smiled at Steve's downcast face.

He brightened up. "That's right. And when we start our businesses, we can help each other if we run into difficulties."

This, also, was not exactly what she'd had in mind, but she didn't want to spoil his good mood by disagreeing. They continued to chat about their respective start-ups during the meal and before the evening was over, Angela and Steve had decided on another dinner date where they could continue sharing their plans.

That night, at home, Angela decided that having Steve as a friend was fine. As a boyfriend—not. But there was no reason why they shouldn't continue to have the odd dinner now and then together.

Travis put down his paintbrush and stretched. He looked out at the wintry Alberta foothills that were visible through the large picture window of his apartment. It was his favourite scene which never failed to inspire him. He looked again at the little photo taped to his easel. It showed a beautiful woman, her dark-hair disheveled and falling over her bare shoulders that glistened with moisture from recent exertion. Travis's body always reacted with the knowledge of what this "exertion" had been. Her face glowed with secret pleasure, and deep satisfaction shone from her dark eyes. Her luscious full lips, gleaming with the afterglow of his ardent kisses, were slightly parted, as though begging to be kissed again.

The portrait of Angela which Travis had been painting for several weeks was nearly complete, only missing a few strokes on the background. He was satisfied with his work, which brought him almost masochistic pleasure. He couldn't help gazing at her, although this brought on the pain of knowing he would never see her again.

There was a knock on the door of his walk-up apartment. He was expecting his friend, John Garth, to drop by. Travis had told John that he had begun to paint again, and John had wanted to come over and take a look at what Travis had produced. Being in the advertising business, John was always on the look-out for something he could possibly convey into an ad.

"It's open!" Travis called.

After shucking off his winter jacket, John walked around the apartment, inspecting the canvasses that were set up for display on the floor, against the walls, and on chairs.

"Great work," John commented.

"Thanks," Travis said.

"So what are you doing there?" John came over to the easel and bent his tall, lanky frame over to look more closely at the painting of Angela. He gave a low whistle.

Travis was uncomfortable having John gawking at the painting of Angela. "Oh, I'm just finishing it," he said carelessly, and quickly detached the photo from the easel and slipped it into his pocket. He hadn't meant for John—or anyone else for that matter—to see Angela kneeling on the bed with her dark hair flowing on her glistening shoulders, and those lips . . . so thoroughly kissed! It was *his* memory and his only.

"I think this is excellent!" John crowed. "I knew you were a good painter, but I didn't know you were *this* good!" He continued to inspect the picture. "No offense, but I mean since you don't usually paint."

"No offense taken," Travis replied. "I haven't painted much in the last few years, though I used to paint all the time before I took up landscape designing. It pays better," he said with a chuckle. "And now I just paint as a hobby, because I don't seem to have much time for it."

"This is really fabulous," John continued to enthuse. "May I take a picture of it?"

And before Travis had a chance to reply, John had snapped a photo of the painting with his iPhone. "So who *is* this dark-haired beauty?" he asked.

"Oh, it's just a woman I met on the cruise last summer. Pretty, isn't she?"

John whistled again. "I would say she is! Where does she live?"

"In Toronto. I haven't seen her since the cruise. And unfortunately we're not in touch, either." Travis grimaced. Yes, that was unfortunate, for sure.

"Why not?" John inspected the painting up close. "Me, I think I would've made sure I at least had her e-mail address."

"We never got that far. It just didn't happen." And Travis knew for a fact that Angela wouldn't have replied even if he had every possible contact information on her—e-mail, phone number, postal address, Facebook—whatever.

"Bummer. But maybe it's for the best." John threw himself into a black leather armchair. "Toronto is pretty far away for carrying on an affair."

"I could have flown there to see her every few weeks," Travis said. He'd often thought about how the long-distance relationship could have worked out—if there had been one. But since there wasn't, it was a moot point. "My mom lives in Toronto, you know," he added, to give some substance to his words.

But John had already lost interest in the topic and picked up a magazine. "Did you see the ad I created for this make-up firm, 'Beauty Plus'? They liked my idea so much they want me to cook up some more ads for them."

Travis clapped his friend on the shoulder. "Hey, that's great, John. That's a pretty decent client you've got yourself. That should get your advertising business shooting off the ground."

John grinned. "Yeah. I already have a great idea for their mascara line. And I'm thinking what to do for the eyeliner and lipstick ads. Now if I just managed to get another couple of clients like this, I'll be hiring designers."

"Right. Dream big, buddy." Yeah, just like he was dreaming big, thinking that maybe some day he would run into Angela and she would listen to him and then . . . Forget it. It wasn't ever going to happen. That was a futile dream. And, besides, by now Angela had probably found someone to love.

Chapter Seven

Angela and Steve walked along the snowy downtown street on their way to the Golden Plum, where they now regularly went for dinner together. Though "regularly" was hardly the word, it being only the third time they were meeting. They had decided that Thursdays would be their dinner cum discussion nights.

The restaurant was full, for Christmas shoppers also had to eat, but they managed to get a table in the centre of the room. Steve looked very uncomfortable, and Angela, also, didn't like the location of the table. She felt almost like they were sitting in a display window, but they had no other choice.

"Maybe we should have gone to another restaurant," Steve muttered, sitting with his shoulders hunched while scanning the familiar menu. "Let's just order something fast and get out of here."

Angela laughed. "We're not trying to hide from anybody, are we? I admit I'm not fond of sitting in the middle of the room, either, but surely we can put up with it this once."

Steve mumbled something in reply and signaled for the waitress to come and get their orders.

Angela shrugged and went along with him, though she couldn't help feeling slightly amused by his attitude. It was as though he was afraid of being seen. They both ordered soup and sandwiches which wouldn't take long, and ate quickly.

Travis opened the door of the Golden Plum and entered with his mother on his arm. The place was full with late-night shoppers looking for dinner and there were several people already lined up for tables.

"Ten minutes," the hostess said and took Travis's name down.

They sat on a bench to wait and idly he scanned the room. All at once he started. Angela! Sitting there in the company of a man. He didn't look Spanish so obviously he wasn't her brother. For a few minutes Travis stared, his heart thumping loudly in his breast. Memories of the afternoon in his cabin had never left him and now, seeing her, they came back with a vengeance.

"What is it, dear," Mrs. Jordan asked. "You look like you've seen a ghost."

"It's nothing. I just thought I saw someone," he replied, hoping his voice didn't expose his agitated state.

"I'm sorry. Did you say you *thought* you saw some-one, or you actually *saw* someone?" his mother asked.

Travis swallowed. What should he say? His percep-tive mother would surely hear if he lied. "I saw some-one."

"And does this someone have a name?" Mrs. Jordan persisted.

"Angela," Travis coughed out hoarsely.

"Angela? Isn't that the beautiful lady in those pic-tures from your cruise?"

"Yes." He cursed his mother's great memory. How could she remember the name of someone she had never met, from just having seen her photo several months ago?

"Well, that is wonderful! What a coincidence. Shall we go and say hello?"

Travis stood up. "Mom, I think we'll just look for an-other restaurant," he said offering his hand to his mother. "Let's go."

"But the hostess said it's only ten minutes," his mother objected. "I can wait that long."

"I can't," he said curtly, causing his mother's eye-brows to raise.

"Fine," she said, also getting up, "If you're *that* hun-gry."

Outside the restaurant Travis took deep gulps of the

crisp, wintry air to calm himself. Yes, he had known Angela lived in Toronto, but in a city of millions, what were the chances of running into her? Of course stranger things happened in the world so this chance meeting was really not such a rare occurrence. It was just an unfortunate one.

But still . . . Travis shook his head. If she had been sitting there by herself, he would have walked over to speak to her, even if the reception would more than likely have been chilly. Probably frozen, like today's weather. But since she was sitting with a boyfriend— or a husband?—he wasn't going to go there and inter- rupt their dinner.

He sighed. She was such a wonderful woman and he had blown it big time. Although, really there was no way he could have won, whether he had lied or told the truth. Taking his mother by the arm, he led her down the sidewalk toward another restaurant. One that didn't have Angela sitting in it.

Before half an hour had passed, Angela and Steve had finished eating and were standing on the side- walk, trying to decide what they would do now. They had done very little talking during the hurried meal and had both just slurped their soups down quickly.

"Well, that was a speedy dinner," Angela said. "I think we should call it a night."

"Yeah," Steve agreed. "I have to get up early to go to

a job, anyway."

"And since it's so close to Christmas and everyone is busy, let's agree to call this our last dinner." she suggested.

"Till next year," Steve said, "I'll call you in January."

But Angela had already made up her mind that this would be their last meeting. The dinners would not continue beyond tonight but, as always, she was loathe to cause him distress and tell him so directly.

Instead she turned her face away as he bent to kiss her.

Christmas shopping was in full swing. Angela came out of a toy store, her arms laden with bags and parcels. Why were toys always boxed up in such huge containers? She decided to call it a day for she had no more fingers left to hold another bag. She had come downtown on the subway, rather than bring her car into this madhouse, and now she got ready to hail a cab to take her home.

Throngs of people passed her, some jostling her packages as she stood near the curb, arm half-raised in readiness should a taxi come along. Just then a man with two small children passed by and her arm dropped in surprise.

Steve! He was holding two little girls by the hand. His sister's kids, flashed through Angela's mind, while at the same moment she remembered him saying his sister had no children. Who were they then?

Before she could call out to him, she heard one of the little girls whine, "Daddy, I wanna go home *now*. I'm tired."

Angela's jaw dropped. Wha-at?

"Stop complaining," the man growled. "You wanted to come shopping for Mommy, so now . . ." The trio was swallowed by the crowds and were out of earshot.

Frozen to the spot, Angela stood for a full minute on the curb. Then she snapped into action. Maybe that wasn't Steve, but some look-alike family man. With Steve's voice? Whom was she kidding! It was Steve, all right. And she was going to get to the bottom of this.

With the bags of toys bouncing against her hips and bumping other pedestrians, she hurried after them, hoping Steve and the children hadn't gone into some store. No, they hadn't, because after a few moments she saw them ahead of her.

Soon she could hear the little girl whimper again, "Daddy, let's go *home*. I wanna go home *now*."

And then she was right behind them. She reached out and poked Steve on the arm with a free finger. "Steve! I thought it was you," she exclaimed, pretending to be pleasantly surprised.

Steve whirled around and his face turned the colour of Rudolph's nose. "Angela," he croaked.

"So you are Christmas shopping with your . . .?"

There was no response from him, but his mouth kept opening and closing in such a funny way, Angela could hardly hold back her laughter.

"And these little girls must be . . .?" She kept her voice as innocent and natural as possible.

Steve seemed to have difficulty getting a sound out of his mouth, so the older girl spoke up. "I'm Chrissy and this is my sister Caroline. We're shopping for a gift for Mommy, but Caroline wants to go home. She's always such a *whiner*."

"Am *not*!" the smaller girl riposted. "I'm just tired. That's all."

Angela forced herself to laugh in the delighted way adults do when children are being cute. "So what were you going to get for Mommy?" she asked the older girl, who seemed to be a real fount of information. All this time she didn't look at Steve. She wasn't sure whether she would laugh at him or slap him in the face, but she knew she wouldn't be able to keep up this cheerful banter if she looked at him. Besides, slapping him in front of his children would not be cool.

"Daddy already got her a silk scarf, but Caroline and I wanted to get her something from us, too."

"Chocolates!" Caroline piped up.

This time Angela's laughter was genuine. "Chocolates! I bet Mommy would like that."

"Yes, she would," Caroline said. "An' she'd give me some of them, too."

"I'm sure she would," Angela said. "But what does the silk scarf look like that Daddy got for Mommy?" She suspected she already knew, and was sure Chrissy would confirm her suspicions. She was right.

"It's got kind of like soft spring colours," Chrissy said. "It's very pretty, but I don't know if Mommy will like it. She doesn't usually wear clothes that colour."

"Right." She now looked at Steve. "Seems to me I have seen a scarf like that . . . somewhere?" Angela couldn't help it if the devil made her say that.

Steve's face couldn't get any more flushed. He looked so ridiculous that Angela suddenly felt totally cool and calm. She wasn't going to slap him because the man wasn't worth it. He meant less than nothing to her and his deceitful shenanigans didn't affect her one bit.

"So where's Mommy now?" she asked Crissy.

"She's at home. She's got so much work to do she threw us out so we'd be out of her way," Chrissy revealed, laughing

Angela looked directly into Steve's eyes but he couldn't keep eye-contact with her for more than a fleeting second. "The poor woman," she said, as though in response to Chrissy's words, but she knew Steve got her message.

"Let's go *home*," Caroline whined again.

Angela patted the child's colourful wool toque. "I know how you feel," she said. "I want to go home, too, so I'll be on my way. You all have a great Christmas and I hope Santa brings you lots of lovely presents. Oh, and please say hello to Mommy from Daddy's dear friend, Angela."

Okay, so maybe she shouldn't have said that. It might cause problems in the obviously troubled marriage. Or, who knew, maybe Steve kept his wayward moves so well hidden that poor Mommy had no idea she didn't have his love all to herself. Who knew.

Angela turned to face the traffic and just then a taxi approached. She raised her arm and it stopped to pick her up. As she sat in the back, she couldn't stop shaking with fury. But the anger was directed at herself, not at Steve.

What a gullible idiot she had been! Again!

Easter was approaching and Angela stood like a mannequin in the display window of her little boutique. Down came the heavy wool sweaters, the little sled on a white fluffy carpet and the snowman made from balls of white yearn. She took up the "snow" and replaced it with a carpet of "grass". On it she positioned a couple of big soft white bunnies and several balls of yarn in happy spring colours that stood for Easter eggs.

"Hand me the flowers, please," she said and reached back. Sylvia placed silk tulips and daffodils into her outstretched hand and Angela arranged them into little clusters which she placed here and there on the grass.

Sylvia slipped outside to take a look at the new display and soon popped her head back in through the door. "Your display looks gorgeous!" she enthused. "You're getting to be very creative with your yarns. No one can walk by without looking at this window. Come and see for yourself."

Angela joined Sylvia out on the sidewalk to take in the effect and nodded. "Yes, I think it looks very colourful and spring-like." The marquee above the door read, "Woolly Bear Yarns and Knits" and on it crawled a very eye-catching black Woolly Bear caterpillar, sporting a rusty stripe across its fat tummy. "All the display needs are a few Woolly Bears crawling around on the grass."

"That'll be so cute!" Sylvia exclaimed. "Where will you get them?"

"I'm making them out of wool, of course. I'll do a few tonight while I watch TV."

They re-entered the shop and Angela took her place behind the counter as two ladies walked in. They inspected the books of patterns that Angela had created and fingered the soft cardigans that were on display around the boutique.

"I'd like to order this design for my daughter's birth-day," one of the ladies said, pointing to an intricate pattern. "When could you have it ready?"

Angela wrote down the details of the order and the women left. She then phoned one of her knitters who would get the job done by the agreed upon date.

As she hung up, Sylvia emerged from the back with two cups of tea.

"I'm not too happy with all this TV watching you are doing," Sylvia preached. "You're spending way too many evenings at home."

"Sylvia, you know I've been extremely busy with this shop," Angela exclaimed. "It takes a lot of energy. And when I haven't been here, working, I've sat at home knitting my little fingers to the bone."

"That's true," Sylvia conceded. "I was mainly be-moaning your lack of dates."

Angela waved her hand dismissively. "I have no time for dates. And I do not need a husband to complete me, if that's where this lecture is heading. You are married and that's fine for you. But it is not for every-one. Like me, for example."

"That's true, too." Sylvia put down her teacup and got up out of her chair to give Angela a hug. "I just want you to be as happy in a relationship as I am with Jeff."

"Thank you, Sylvia. I know you mean it. But after two disappointing relationsh—" Too late she realized her mistake and broke off, but not before Sylvia's eyebrows had lifted in surprise.

"Two?"

"I meant one, of course," Angela quickly amended.

Sylvia eyes her suspiciously. "Since when have you begun to mix up your numbers like that? So it's Cheating Steve and who else?"

Angela turned and went to take her teacup to the back room. "I don't want to talk about it." It was totally uncharacteristic of her to snap at her best friend, but the sudden thought of Travis shook her up.

Sylvia followed her into the kitchen. "Okay. We'll play it your way, but you realize I'm now filled with curiosity that's crying to be appeased."

"That's too bad. Could you please help me pack up these decorations?"

They worked in silence, stuffing the winter displays into boxes, until Sylvia suddenly blurted out, "I suspect the second one is this Travis fellow on the ship. Right?"

"What on earth made you say that?" Angela asked after she was sure her voice would sound normal.

"There has been no other man in the picture for ever so long, that's why." Sylvia sounded too smug and it irritated Angela.

"Travis never was in the picture," she pointed out.

"He was in the pictures from your trip. But there were no other males among your photos that I saw. None that would arouse my suspicion. But, hey, you don't have to tell me about him. I'm just your oldest bestie, that's all."

Angela knew it was no use continuing to deny that nothing had happened between her and Travis. Sylvia was very good at reading between the lines and it was surprising the facts about Travis hadn't surfaced before this.

"Yes," she admitted with a sigh. "He's the other one. But that is all I am going to say about it. Now."

"Oh, dear," Sylvia exclaimed. "I suspect it was a very tragic affair and you are still hurting, so I won't probe."

"Thank you, Sylvia."

"So you really detest him?" Sylvia rinsed out the tea cups under hot running water in the sink.

Angela picked up one of the cardboard boxes and headed for the door. She would have to store the display material in the house. As she headed out to her car, she thought about what Sylvia had asked. Detest him? Did she? It was more like a huge disappointment she felt. Disappointment that a man whom she had grown so fond of—she did not want to say "fallen in love with"—had turned out to be such a moral Pygmy whose wife had meant so little to him.

Of course the same could be said for Steve, who also disrespected his wife and—incredibly—his two sweet daughters. But for Steve she felt only contempt, and she pitied his poor family. For Travis—there was no comparison. Despite his actions, she couldn't help the ache that still lingered inside her heart whenever she thought of him. If she ever came face-to-face with him, she had no idea what her reaction would be. Would she confront him angrily or would she simply ignore him? Luckily, with him living almost three thousand kilometres away near the foothills of the Rockies, there was only a tiny chance in the great vastness of the universe for them to meet. It would be very difficult for him to locate her—if he even wanted to—and she had no desire to find *him*. That was for sure!

Angela sighed and stuffed the box in the trunk of her car. She returned into the shop and snagged a towel from the hook by the stove.

"Sylvia, you said you would not pry. And I really don't want to talk about him," she said and began to dry the cups. "I hope you'll do me the courtesy of not mentioning his name again. At least not till I'm ready to say something. If ever I am."

Sylvia nodded. "I promise."

Angela made an effort to brighten up. "I'm so happy that my little shop is starting to pick up customers," she said to change the subject, "It gives me such satisfaction to look around this boutique. I already have several regulars who come to buy wool for their own projects, and ask for advice. And I have sold lots of my own pattern booklets, not to mention many of the sweaters that have been on display." Some of them she had knit herself, some were made by her very talented knitters. She pirouetted around in the little space that was available for dancing. "Can you tell I'm bursting with pride?"

Sylvia smiled. "And well you should be. I'm pleasantly surprised how well the business has got off the ground."

"I think where it's situated has a lot to do with it. You were very astute when you suggested a more high-end location. People who live here appreciate handmade products and they spread the word. One day I even had a lady from Vancouver who had discovered the shop on my website. When she came to visit her friend here in Toronto, she came to check me out. She loved the store and is already a regular customer, ordering wool and patterns for herself. She even wants to open a similar business in Vancouver. Do you think maybe 'Woolly Bear Yarns and Knits' could become a franchise?"

"Angela, I think you can do anything you set your mind to," Sylvia cried and gave her friend a warm hug. "Success is your middle name."

Except in love.

Summer had arrived. Angela kept herself so busy with the boutique that she had no time to think of anything else. Or anyone else.

Except at night. Her fickle dreams would not leave her alone and kept her tossing and turning, waking her up with a pounding heart. In the dreams Travis was always his companionable, funny and caring self, the way he was on the ship. Too bad his deceitful secret had spoiled everything beautiful they had experienced on the cruise.

Another Monday morning and another sleepless night. Angela unlocked the back door of her boutique which opened onto a small alleyway where she parked her car. She quickly dispensed with the usual morning routines and promptly at nine o'clock she unlocked the front door and turned her sign to OPEN. This always made her feel such a sense of pride. Sometimes she wondered if Steve had got his painting business off the ground, but that thought never occupied her mind for more than a few seconds. She simply didn't care one way or the other.

Around noon she took a few bites of the sandwich she had brought from home, along with a cup of tea. She heard the door open with the jingle of a little brass bell that was above the door, and she hid the sandwich under the counter. With her back turned to the shop she gave her mouth a quick wipe with a serviette and then pivoted to face the customer. Or rather his back, for the customer was a man, which was surprising, for not that many men ever walked in through the door of her wool shop. As he inspected the display of sweaters, it seemed to Angela there was something familiar about him.

Travis! Angela's hand flew to her mouth to suffocate the audible gasp. She stared at his back, hoping it was a hallucination that would disappear if she blinked. It didn't.

A few moments later he turned to ask a question, but no sound came out of his mouth which remained open. At last he croaked, "Angela!"

They stared at each other, and from the look on his face, Travis seemed to be just as unable to believe his eyes as she was.

"What are you doing here?" she at last whispered. It was obvious from his surprised face that he hadn't known the shop was hers. Thus it made no sense to ask how he had found her.

"I . . . I'm looking for a sweater for my mother," he explained, his voice hoarse. He coughed. "She lives in Toronto."

"I didn't know that." How come that fact had never come up? One would have though, when she had said she lived in Toronto, he would have mentioned that his mother did, also. Was there some reason he hadn't wanted to divulge that fact? Perhaps so the two could never meet and discuss his wife.

"Yes, she does. I flew from Calgary to celebrate her birthday. It's a biggie—eighty years."

"That's nice."

They stood, facing each other. Angela tried to calm down her pulse that seemed to be stuck on high. Then she saw his features soften.

"How have you been?" he asked, now seeming to be fully in control of himself. His deep voice sounded so gentle, like it had on the ship. But Angela refused to fall for it. Mendacity, that's all it was.

"Fine," she snapped. She was not going to ask him how he was. She simply didn't allow herself care.

"This is your shop?"

God! Did he have to sound so caring.

"Yes." She made sure her voice did not reciprocate his.

"It's very nice. I can see you've put a lot of thought into it. It's cute, while at the same time very efficient-looking."

He could stop this flattery any time. She didn't want to hear any of it.

"Thank you." Was she being off-putting enough?

He approached her, and Angela was thankful she

was behind the counter. He stopped a couple of metres from her and his hand made a move toward her. "I never thought I would ever find you. Although I did see you in a restaurant before Christmas."

That was a surprise that left her gaping. "You did?"

"Yes. I came to spend Christmas with my mother, and we were going to have lunch at the Golden Plum. It was full, and we were waiting to get a table. You were there, sitting with a man. Your husband?"

By now Angela was totally off guard. "I have no husband," she blurted out.

"Boyfriend then?"

She had no intention of sharing her life with him, but against her best-laid plans she replied, "I have no boyfriend."

His face brightened considerably. "I'm happy to hear that."

This brought her back to reality. "Why?" she snapped. "What difference does it make?"

Her question seemed to confuse him. "Because . . . because I'm so glad to have found you. Again."

"Stranger things have happened." Yes, she was forcing herself to be rude, even if that was totally against everything she had ever been taught.

"I am delighted to see you," he went on.

"Are you?"

"Don't you believe me?"

"What does it matter what I believe, Travis? I never wanted to see you again after . . ." She caught herself in time. She wanted to tell him to leave, but somehow those words refused to come out. Instead she turned around to face the colourful balls of yarn on the shelves behind the counter. The playful sight brought her no pleasure.

Angela could sense him coming closer and was doubly thankful for the counter that separated them. She wished there was more room for her to step away, but her nose was already almost against the balls of yarn.

"Angela, we need to talk. I want to explain—"

At that moment the brass bell jingled and a woman entered the shop. Angela whirled around to face her, a smile of welcome on her face, and Travis backed away from the counter and went to inspect the sweaters again.

The customer pulled out a pattern from her handbag and showed it to Angela. "I don't particularly like the colours they are using in this pattern, but I love the pattern itself," she informed Angela. She looked at Travis. "This gentleman was here before me?"

Travis shook his head. "No, it's all right. I'm still looking."

The lady took her time choosing several colours of yarn for a vest she was knitting and Angela helped her with the multitude of choices. Half an hour later

Angela rang up the purchases and the lady left with her bags of wool. She smiled at Travis with satisfaction as she walked past him. "I hope you weren't in a hurry," she said.

"No problem," he replied.

Angela remained behind the counter, her insides shaking with trepidation.

But before Travis could approach her, another customer entered, and after her, another. Angela was grateful for their presence for, as was often the case in the yarn shop, the women took a long time making their selections.

Travis stood, endlessly circling the shop and fingering the sweaters on display. At last he looked down at his watch. "Excuse me," he said over the head of a woman who was assiduously counting her change. "I have to run, but I'll be back tomorrow."

"Right," Angela said while holding out her palm to receive the coins the woman handed her. The word could have been addressed to either person. "Thank you very much." She handed the lady the bags with the Wooly Bear logo on them, and Travis courteously held open the door to the customer while looking at Angela.

"I'll be back," he repeated.

The brass bell jingled softly as the door closed behind him.

In the little back room Angela made herself a cup of tea to calm her pounding heart. What were the chances of him walking into her shop to choose a gift for his mother? Impossible! And, yet—it had just happened.

Chapter Eight

The following morning was slow and to Angela the little boutique began to feel like a torture chamber from which she couldn't escape. Was Travis really coming? When? As the hours crawled by and lunch time approached, she began to hope that maybe he had changed his mind and wasn't coming after all. Yes, he had told her he had to run somewhere and was coming back. But maybe, after unwittingly stepping into the shop, he had looked for a way to extricate himself from an awkward situation by saying he had to go. It had probably just been a convenient way to make an exit. So why wouldn't he just have looked at his watch and got out, instead of saying he wanted to explain something.

Angela set her teacup down on the counter. Enough of this ridiculous speculation! These kinds of thoughts could drive her mad. She took a bite of her sandwich and just then the bell jingled and door of the boutique opened. She almost choked.

Travis stepped in and without any how-de-do he crossed the room with a purposeful step. "Angela, we need to talk," he said firmly and leaned his palms on the counter.

She backed away but the shelves behind her prevented her from getting far enough from the face that was set with a determined scowl.

"Now," he said.

She couldn't move. Taking sideways steps to escape into the back room didn't seem to be the wisest thing to do, for she knew he would follow. And then where could she go? Run into the alley?

His face softened and he heaved himself up to sit on the counter. "I had to leave yesterday because my Mom was expecting me. But I need to tell you something. I don't know if that will make any difference in how you see me as a person, but I have to try."

Travis was too close. Angela couldn't get a sound out of her constricted throat. And, besides, what was there to say?

"All this time I've been thinking about what happened that afternoon," he began.

Angela could feel her face getting hot and put up a hand as if to protect herself from what she knew would follow. "Please don't," she whispered.

"I can't blame you for feeling my behaviour was

despicable. And I guess in a way it was. Elaine had only just died and here I was, making love to the first beautiful woman whom I met. But I swear I didn't expect that to happen. It never was my intention. Not in a hundred years."

Angela looked down at her hands that were trembling. She clutched them into fists to prevent him from seeing her turbulent reaction.

"I haven't been able to get peace, thinking about how you looked at me when you left. That look of disdain in your eyes, it's been with me ever since. And now I want to explain what was going on in my life—"

"Please, you don't have to explain." The words came out hoarse and Angela had to cough. "There's nothing—"

"Yes, there is, but—"

The brass bell jingled softly and Travis slid off the counter. Angela had never been so happy to see a customer walk in.

After lengthy conversation and at least twenty minutes of hemming and hawing, the woman at last left, happy with her yarns and satisfied with her choice of colours. Meanwhile Travis wandered around the shop, looking again and again at the selection of sweaters.

"I can see this isn't the best place to carry on this conversation," Travis said. "What time do you close?"

"At six. But I don't—"

"Angela, since the fates have unexpectedly granted me this opportunity to talk to you, please let me have a few minutes of your time. I promise I won't ever bother you again if only you'll le me explain. It may not make any difference in how you think of me, but it will give me peace of mind to know you've heard my side of the story. May I come at six and take you for dinner?"

Angela nodded. Travis left, but after only a moment he returned, grinning his familiar smile. "While I'm here, I might as well pick up that sweater for my mom, which was my reason for coming into your shop in the first place. Will you help me choose something pretty?"

Angela was reluctant to go near him and be so close to his masculine presence but she was, after all, the shopkeeper and he was a customer. She couldn't help feeling that he was procrastinating, taking much too long looking at the sweater selection. It was almost as though he wanted to prolong their close contact. But when another customer walked into the shop, he made a quick decision and picked a cashmere cardigan in a soft blue tone. Again, Angela had the feeling he had made this choice much earlier, but had only kept looking in order to stay in the store.

She wrapped the sweater in tissue paper with care and slipped it into one of her Wooly Bear boutique bags.

Travis held the bag up, inspecting the logo. "This is really cute," he said. "You know, you've done a wonderful job with this shop. As you're aware, I've had more than a few minutes to look around, and I'm very impressed."

She felt the heat rise to her cheeks, only this time it was from pleasure. "Thank you," she said and couldn't help smiling.

"So this is what you wished for when you blew out your birthday candle on the ship?"

Now Angela had to laugh. "No, nothing this specific. But I hoped I would discover something that would inspire me." Angela waved her arm to take in everything in the shop. "I think I have achieved what I was looking for."

This casual conversation helped her to feel slightly more at ease. So when Travis returned promptly at six to pick her up, she got into his car with only a slight feeling of apprehension. What was he going to reveal that might explain what had happened on the ship? She really couldn't think of anything that would mitigate his actions.

"Elaine was sick with MS for ten years," Travis began after they had settled down at a table and had ordered their meals. "The last eight of them she spent in a nursing home."

"Oh, I'm so sorry."

"Yes, it can be an awful disease. Hers advanced quickly to the stage where she was confined to bed. My work took me away, sometimes for weeks, but I visited her every chance I got and spent every weekend with her."

Angela swallowed. She had a pretty good idea where this was going. Obviously their marriage had been seriously affected by the terrible illness.

"Elaine told me many times not to come to the nursing home any more. In fact she often shouted at me angrily that I must divorce her. She said she wanted me to live a normal life and not be tied to a dying body that was never going to get out of bed."

At his horrible words Angela gasped and her hand flew to her mouth. How Elaine must have suffered during those years of immobility, loving her husband, yet willing to give him up so he could live a normal life. The poor woman. "I'm so very sorry," she whispered.

"Yes. She had told me that after she died and was buried, I should go away and not have to think about coming to the nursing home any more. It so happened that the job in Italy came up just before her death, and so, when she died, I followed her wishes and tacked on the cruise at the end of the work assignment." He stopped and then said, as though defending himself, "I was following her wishes."

"Yes, it seems you were. But was it also her wish

that you should have an affair only weeks after her death?" Angela knew her words were sharp but they revealed the crux of the problem. He had disrespected his wife by sleeping with a woman so soon after her death, and Angela had difficulty dealing with that.

A look of pain flashed across his face. He lowered his eyes and began to cut his steak while Angela waited for his reply without speaking.

At last he looked up. "I swear I never meant for that to happen. In all the years Elaine was ill, I never even considered having anyone else on the side. I was true to her and lived a celibate life. I didn't resent my situation because we had married for better or for worse." He stopped and looked at Angela with his brown eyes. The eyes that had so often bothered her in her dreams, but were now filled with a deep sadness. "I just never imagined that worse would be that bad," he said quietly.

Angela's heart filled with aching empathy for him. His words were those of a man devoted to his wife, a wife who was sick and beyond help. What pain must he have gone through in those years as he watched her slowly die before his eyes.

"Oh, Travis. I'm so very sorry for my harsh words. Please forgive me."

"You had every right to think whatever awful things you thought about me," Travis said and his voice held no censure, as though he was trying to comfort and reassure her.

This made her feel even worse. She wished she would have held back her self-righteous anger on the ship long enough to hear him out.

He now looked directly into her eyes. "In all this time I've not been able to forget you. I thought at first it was because I was bothered by the impression you had of me and my inability to do anything about it. But as time went by, I realized it was because of something else."

Travis reached out a hand to cover hers across the table. Sparks trailed up her arm and spread into every cell of her body. "You filled my thoughts during the day and I dreamt about you at night," he said. "I realized it wasn't a guilty conscience that was the cause. There was something about you that I simply couldn't get you off my mind."

"It is the same with me," Angela whispered. Her days and nights had been filled with thoughts of him because, despite everything, there was something about him she hadn't been able to forget. Perhaps her heart had been trying to tell her that he was not a bad person, but just a man who was in love.

"I believe what occurred between us on the ship was wrought by the Fates," he said. "I don't think either one of us meant for it to happen."

"I think it happened because the whole cruise was like a fairy tale," Angela agreed. "At least for me it was. Remember the storks? And then, sadly, it all evaporated like Brigadoon. It was over, just like you predicted it would be."

"I didn't want that to happen. I had already made up my mind that we would be in touch after the cruise and eventually get together. I just didn't see us getting intimate and . . . " Travis stopped and swallowed. "But I never forgot about you," he went on. "I always carried you in my heart and dreamt of someday meeting you again. Even though I knew the chance of that ever happening was less than zero."

Angela's heart was bursting with happiness. "I can't believe that out of the blue you stepped into my store," she said. "Those kinds of things happen only in movies."

"Or in fairy tales," Travis said, smiling. "Wouldn't you say our story is like a fairy tale? Happy ending and all." His eyes grew dark with desire and his hand grasped hers more tightly. "Angela?" he whispered.

She knew what he was asking, and it was exactly what she wanted, too.

"Yes," she whispered back. A blush rose onto her cheeks at the thought of what this was leading to.

"I'm afraid my mother's home isn't—" he began, but Angela stopped him.

"We will go to my place," she stated. Strangely, she felt no embarrassment at being so forward. Being with Travis again was what she had dreamed of for months, and now it was becoming a reality. It all felt so natural, like it was meant to be.

On the way to her condo in his car Travis kept his hand on her knee, as though wanting to make sure she wouldn't disappear. Angela unlocked her apartment door and held it open for him.

"Nice place," he said taking in the spacious, light apartment. As he removed his jacket and shoes, she could tell his eyes were directed toward the bedroom door.

As she took off her coat and boots, she swallowed in anticipation of what she knew was coming. "Yes, I like it," she said, but her voice was far from sounding confident. She almost had to force the words out, and she was even having difficulty with her breathing. Travis was standing too close.

And then he wasn't just close. She was right in his arms and he was holding her so tightly her breath again had trouble flowing.

"Angela," he murmured against her neck while his hands pulled out the pins and let down her hair. "My darling Angela."

He picked her up in his arms and headed for the bedroom. Gently he lowered her on the queen bed and then stood above her, looking down at her with so much love in his eyes that she felt herself almost drowning in the feeling. Her heart beat quickly and her mouth opened slightly to invite his lips on hers.

Then he bent down to do just that. Their lips fused while their tongues sparred in each other's mouth. Small whimpers came from deep inside her, and she grasped the back of his neck, her fingers pulling his hair, letting him know this was not enough.

His hands began to undress her with a strong urgency that made her squirm under his ministrations. When she lay there naked before his adoring eyes, he stopped and sighed deeply.

"My darling, you are so beautiful," he said softly. "My eyes can't get enough of you."

But the rest of his body obviously wanted its own share, for Angela could see his hard penis pushing against his pants. She tugged on the zipper pull and let it push out, now only impeded by his underwear. She thrust her hand into the slot and pulled it out. The soft velvety tip contrasted with the hard shaft and for a few seconds she caressed it, before pulling it into her mouth.

Travis gasped in delighted surprise and pushed himself against her, as she began to suck, slowly taking him in completely.

It didn't take long before he groaned and convulsed,

as his semen shot into her mouth. Angela swallowed and let it flow down her throat. She was surprised how easy this new act turned out to be.

When Travis had regained his breath he drew himself out of her and removed his clothing.

"I want to lie here next to you, and feel your skin against mine," he whispered. It was as though he didn't want to break the spell of the magical thing that had just taken place.

Angela didn't know how long they lay there, touching each other, arms and legs wrapped around each other. She could hear Travis's breath become calm and then realized he was asleep.

She smiled. Men. She'd heard they often fell asleep after satisfying sex and it was good to know the sex she had given him had satisfied him. After so many lonely months of wishing things could have been different, at last they were. Angela was now fully awake—not dreaming—and, incredibly, Travis was really here, lying beside her.

She kissed the tip of his nose and he opened one eye.

"Are you still there?" he murmured.

"I am." She laughed softly. "Sleeping Beauty is just waiting for her Prince Charming to wake up."

Travis frowned. "Something about that doesn't sound right." He pulled her close and she snuggled against his chest.

"Maybe in our fairy tale things are done differently," Angela said, giving his nipple a little bite.

"Yes, this is our own Brigadoon," he said. "Only ours won't disappear after a hundred years."

He kissed her and nuzzled her neck, sending sweet shivers down her spine. "I missed you more that I could imagine missing anyone. It had to mean something," he said.

"And you were always in my thoughts," she confessed. Neither had used the word "love" but she was sure that described her feelings for him. "Can you stay the night?"

"I told Mom I was meeting a friend and would be late," he said. "But since it's not even close to midnight, and you won't turn into a pumpkin for a while yet, I think we can continue." He reached for her. "But I know she'll worry if I'm not there shortly after midnight."

Angela smiled. "Then we had better hurry before I do turn into a pumpkin, or maybe even one of the other creatures. Do you like mice?"

"If you're the mouse, I love them," Travis said with a deep laugh and played with her breasts.

Angela realized how much she had missed his easy laughter.

But then the laughter died as he suddenly entered her and Angela gasped with delight as his thrusts quickly deepened. He plunged into her with more frenzy, all the while looking intensely into her eyes. He groaned loudly at the very moment her own orgasm shook her, and she saw his eyes close with the power of his coming.

Again they lay, wrapped in each other as their breathing slowly subsided. Protection! Suddenly Angela remembered she had forgotten all about a condom, and he hadn't seemed to have it at the top of his mind, either. But somehow this fact didn't bother her. She trusted that Travis had not had anyone else while they were apart, and as for babies . . . she was almost forty. Small chance for that to happen.

Angela rose and pulled on her dressing gown. "It would have been lovely if you could have stayed for the night," she said petulantly.

"I would, but I can't," Travis said and also got up off the rumpled bed. "Not tonight. I want to make love to you again tomorrow. And all the tomorrows after this. But since I'm here for Mom's birthday, and I'm helping to arrange the party, I'm afraid I have to be a good son and forego my own pleasures."

Angela sat back on the bed to watch him get dressed. There was something so masculine in the way he pulled on his pants and zipped them up.

"I was thinking I'd like to have you come to Mom's birthday party," he said. "What do you think?"

Angela nodded, brightening up. "Yes, that would be nice."

"I'd love it if you two met. So you'll come?"

"Of course I will come. I would love to meet your mother." A sudden sadness filled her. "I only wish you could have met mine."

Travis kissed the top of her head. "I'm sure I would have found her to be a very attractive Spanish lady, just like her daughter."

Angela hesitated for a moment and then asked, "Travis, do you think you would care to join us on the Dio de Muerto and celebrate my mother's life with my brother's family?"

"Of course I will come," he replied. Then he fell silent for so long that Angela became worried. What was wrong?

"Angela," he slowly began. "Would it be all right if we also celebrated Elaine? I realize she wasn't Spanish, but I would like to—"

"Oh, Travis!" Angela cried. "What a beautiful thought. Of course we will include Elaine in our celebrations. I am so happy you proposed it." She got up and kissed him soundly. He really was a good man.

Travis continued to get dressed. He buckled his belt and then reached into his back pocket, where his wallet was. "I almost forgot. I wanted to show you something. Something that's been very precious to me ever since the day I took it." He pulled out a photo and handed it to her. "Remember? I told you it would be my most treasured memory."

"Oh, my," she gasped. It was the photo he had taken of her in his cabin after their lovemaking. Her dark hair, disheveled, fell to her shoulders as she knelt on the bed, her legs tucked under her. Angela blushed at the memory. "I wouldn't want your mother to see this," she said. "Nor anyone else."

He bent down and kissed her mouth. But the soft kiss soon became deeper and she moaned, wanting him again. His body and his hands told her he felt the same and she reached up to pull him onto the bed.

But he released himself with a groan. "God, woman, I want you so much. But I have to go." He slipped his tie around his neck. "Can I pick you up on Sunday about noon for the party?"

"That is three days from now," Angela said with a little pout. "I won't see you till then?"

"I'll drop by the shop after you close and we'll go for dinner. How's that?"

"And what else?" Playfully she flashed open her dressing gown, revealing her breasts.

"That, too, you seductive Carmen!" Travis said with a laugh and kissed the tip of her nose while giving her nipples a quick tweak.

He pulled on his winter jacket and turned to go with

a small salute.

After Travis had left, Angela flopped back on the bed and stretched luxuriously. How wonderful life was! The only problem was the distance between them. They hadn't yet discussed the issue of a long-distance relationship, with everything else they'd had to accomplish today. Angela smiled and ran a finger across her lips that still tingled from his kisses. But surely they could work that out. Right now she couldn't imagine a future without Travis. And she only hoped he felt the same.

Guests milled around the party room where Travis had helped to arrange his mother's birthday party. He looked around the room with satisfaction. He and his siblings had invited as many of her old friends as possible—those who could still maneuver around on their own two feet. There were fewer of these old friends these days, of course, and several had been brought by their children, whom Travis knew because of the years of friendship between their parents. Some young people had come to honour their old friend, even if their parents no longer were around.

His young nieces and nephews added to the general noise with their high-pitched voices as they ran around the spacious party room. Travis knew his mother loved all this attention and sat in her easy

chair like a queen on a throne, receiving congratula-
tions and best wishes, as well as many hugs and
kisses.

And, best of all, Angela was here, too. Although he
was busy with his role as one of the hosts, he kept an
eye on her to see she was always occupied with someone, and her hands were never devoid of snacks or a
drink. It pleased him the way she went often to chat
with his mother. She had told him she'd taken care of
her own mother for years, which was probably why she
could relate so well to older people. Whatever they were
now discussing seemed to amuse his mother im-
mensely, for her eyes sparkled and she was laughing
heartily. Travis had told her that Angela was the
woman who had been in the restaurant before Christmas, and whom he had met on the cruise. With that
he had left his mother to draw her own conclusions
about their relationship.

By six o'clock all the guests, except for Angela, had
departed and most signs of the party had been cleared
away. Travis had asked her to wait for him so he could
take her home. While he paid the caterer, she chatted
with his brother and his wife who were trying to herd
their three kids together.

Angela laughed at their efforts to put a jacket on the
youngest. "I have two nephews," she told them.
"They're a bit younger, but they're twins, so I imagine

my brother and his wife will have their hands full when the munchkins are old enough to run around and resist getting dressed."

The way she related to every member of his family from the oldest to the youngest added to the positive impact Angela was making tonight. Not only on his mother and siblings, but on Travis himself.

He slipped an arm around her shoulders as they walked to his car. "So what did you think of my family?"

"I think your mom is delightful," Angela told him with a smile. "She is so full of life and curiosity. She wanted to know everything about my wool shop and thought the sweater you gave her is lovely. After all her praises I was proud to be able to tell her it was knit from one of my own patterns. Your sister said she is going to come and see what products I have in the store for children. And your mom asked if I would like to come over sometime for tea."

The summer evening was still light and they drove to the shore of Lake Ontario to take in the breeze that drifted across the water. Travis held her hand as they walked along the boardwalk. What a treasure this woman was. To think he had lost her and then, miraculously, had found her again. He hoped she would eventually see that, despite what had happened on the cruise, he was really a good guy. A responsible man.

And would be a very loving husband.

Because after tonight he knew, beyond any doubt, that he loved her and wanted to ask her to marry him.

Chapter Nine

The Arrivals floor at Lester B. Pearson airport was bustling with people, most of whom were probably waiting just as impatiently as Angela. She kept her eyes on the wide glass doors that kept opening and closing as passengers hurried out with their luggage. Many were dressed in shorts and colourful t-shirts, indicating they had been on a holiday to some hot, southern island, while the people waiting for them had on their fall jackets. Many even were wearing raincoats, for the autumn day was cool and rainy. But there was no rain in Angela's heart as she waited impatiently. No Travis yet. It was difficult to keep her anxiety in check and she kept re-checking the overhead Arrivals board to reassure herself that the "Landed" sign after his flight number hadn't been changed to "Delayed".

It seemed like forever since he left after his mother's birthday party, although in reality it was only two months. Two long, lonely months! Whenever the brass bell jingled in her shop, her heart skipped a beat, for she couldn't help hoping that perhaps Travis might surprise her and show up unannounced. On some days, when the thoughts of him overtook her, it had been difficult to concentrate on her work.

She had told Sylvia about how surprised she had been when Travis—the handsome man on the cruise with the monkeys—had walked into her boutique, looking for a gift for his mother. But she had never mentioned how she felt about him. She had only said that they had connected after all and were enjoying the time together, reliving the days on the cruise.

After all, the word "love" had never even been whispered between them, so Angela couldn't be sure that anything would ever come of this relationship—no matter how intense it was at this point in time. Always, at the back of her mind, there was the nagging thought that she really had no idea of how Travis still felt about Elaine. Maybe his dead wife was, and always would be, his one and only true love, and no matter how well he and Angela got along, perhaps no one would ever be able to replace Elaine in his heart.

Although Angela tried not to think about this, sometimes she couldn't help it, and then her heart ached with the uncertainty of it all. She knew that even in the animal world there were some species that mated only once, so it could very well also be true of some human relationships.

During the last two months they had communicated by e-mail, by phone, by Skype and even by snail-mail. In fact Travis had told her what he loved best was to see her hand-writing on an envelope in his mailbox. But in all their correspondence neither of them had ever used the word "love", not even as a closing for an e-mail or a letter. Somehow it didn't seem right, since they had never told about such feelings to each other face to face. The sex they'd had was wonderful, and being away from him for two months was pure torture. She knew was in love with him, but what were his feelings for her?

Angela's brow puckered as she mused about this. Maybe Elaine was irreplaceable in his heart and that was why Travis hadn't ever used the word "love" with Angela. She knew he was fond of her but maybe he didn't feel as deeply about her as he had felt about Elaine. Maybe Angela somehow didn't measure up. She knew with every fibre of her being that he was the only man she would ever love, so it was a most disconcerting thought, to be unsure if his feelings reciprocated hers.

Just then the double glass doors spread open once again and Travis walked out among a throng of hurrying passengers. She floated into his waiting arms with an almost imperceptible whimper.

"I missed you so," she whispered, when her mouth was free to speak again.

"I couldn't wait to hold you," Travis muttered and kissed her again. "Let's get the hell out of here so I can have my way with you."

Angela laughed. "Sex, is that all you care about?" she teased with a mock pout, while her body was already anticipating his caresses. She picked up his hand luggage while he grabbed his large suitcase and maneuvered it onto the escalator.

"No, it's sex with *you* that's all I care about, and just thinking about it, I'm already rising along with this slow escalator," Travis muttered quietly so people behind them wouldn't hear.

Angela's laughter rang out and all thoughts of Elaine vanished as they hurried to her waiting car.

On the way home, driving along the expressway, Angela tried to contain her excitement at the thought of what was waiting for them once they got to her condo.

And her expectations came true a hundred-fold. As soon as they were through the door, Travis picked her up into his arms and, without even removing his jacket or giving her a chance to take off her coat, he marched into the bedroom.

"First things first," he muttered and placed her onto

the bed on her back. He heaved himself beside her and then just lay there for several minutes, holding her tight, his face against her throat. "I just want to feel you close to me, and know that you're really here," he whispered.

Slowly he began to move, first unbuttoning her light overcoat and then her blouse, exposing her bra. This he slipped up without undoing the clasps, and brought her firm breasts for his lips to adore.

"You are so beautiful," he breathed, as his fingers manipulated the taut nipples. He then gathered up the hem of her short skirt and pushed it up, to view her pale blue panties. His hand clasped her crotch and he sighed deeply.

"There lies my treasure," he said. "Under these lovely silky panties. But first could I ask you to get up so I can remove your coat?"

Angela smiled. "I was wondering when you were going to get to that."

Travis got up and extended his hand to her. "It probably *is* easier with all these outer layers removed," he said and gave her one of his wide grins.

They both removed their coats and then Angela slipped out of her blouse, while he shrugged off his shirt and pulled off his tie.

"I had to see a client before boarding, which is why I'm so formally attired," he explained. "But in my suitcase there are more comfortable clothes which I'll put on right after—" He took her in his arms and held her tightly. "Right after I have given you concrete evidence of how much I have missed you." And without another word he quickly took off her remaining clothes, removed his own, and tipped her back onto the bed.

"This time," Angela reminded him, "We will use protection because we don't want to tempt the fates. After our last rather careless encounter I was a bit apprehensive, but nothing came of it."

Their lovemaking was passionate but at the same time considerate of each other. Angela touched him in all the places and in all the ways that she knew brought him the greatest pleasure.

Travis, in turn, showed that he knew exactly where her most erotic spots were, and didn't hesitate to rub and manipulate them until she cried out with pleasure. And when he entered her, he seemed to know just how much friction she could take before she was ready to climax. She heard him cry out her name as he joined her in a shuddering orgasm.

After it was over, they lay sated, arms and legs wrapped around each other, their moist bodies glued together.

Before Travis dozed off, Angela suggested they go and shower together, bringing on a deep grumbling from him.

"Do I have to detach myself from you?" he growled. "Can't we just stay like this forever?"

""My left leg has gone to sleep," Angela announced. "It's been under you long enough."

"Spoilsport," Travis said began to unglue himself from her. "We really are stuck together. Even my penis is still inside you. Couldn't we leave it there until it's time to have another round?"

Angela laughed, and pulled her breasts away from his chest. "Ouch!" she cried "Careful! We *are* glued together!"

In the shower they soaped each other, running their hands over every part, which almost led to more lovemaking. Only the absence of a condom prevented them from carrying this out.

After they were dressed, Angela began to prepare a late evening snack and Travis, standing behind her, told about the turbulent flight and grumbled about the lack of food on it.

He put his arms around her waist and kissed the top of her head. "Call me sex-obsessed, but I want you again."

She pushed him off and shoved a plate of tuna sandwiches into his hands. "Here. This should take your mind off sex."

Travis bit her earlobe. "Never! But I'll take it just to

make you happy."

As he ate Angela sat at the table opposite him and rested her chin in her hands. It was so wonderful to have him there, so lively and full of words. The apartment seemed to come alive when he was in it.

Afterwards as they sat on the couch she snuggled against him while his arm was securely around her shoulders. She had lit a couple of candles that now glowed in the darkening summer evening. The radio played softly in the background, and Angela marveled at the complete and utter peace that filled her.

She recognized the Chopin *Nocturne* on the radio and began to hum along with the group that was singing it. "No heart should refuse love," she sang softly.

"That's nice," Travis said playing with her long hair, which she had allowed to remain free after the shower.

Was it true what the words said? That after having lost love, it was possible to love again. How did he feel about it?

"Did you hear the lyrics, Travis?" she asked.

"Yes, I did," he replied quietly.

"Is that true?" Her heart was pounding. Everything depended on his answer.

"Are you asking if I'm ready to love again?" He had turned her face toward him and was looking directly into her eyes.

"Yes." Her reply came out in a whisper.

"Yes, I'm ready to love again. But only if the woman is you."

A sudden burst of happiness slammed through her. "Oh, Travis, I do love you so much!" she breathed and was immediately swept back into his arms.

"I've been waiting so long to hear you say that," he said, his voice thick with emotion. "I was afraid that deep down you still despised me for what happened on the cruise."

"For a long time I did," she confessed. "I couldn't let go of the thought that you had disrespected Elaine. But at the same time, I couldn't stop thinking about you."

"I must admit that at first I couldn't help feeling uneasy about what we were doing, even though it was so wonderful and was happening almost of its own volition. But I knew in my heart Elaine wouldn't have held it against me, so in the end I knew I hadn't done anything wrong."

"I refused to listen to you when you tried to explain the situation to me," Angela said. "I'm so sorry. We wasted almost a whole year because of that. As the song said, our hearts had lost their way. I tremble just to think what my life would be like now if you hadn't come into my shop."

"My heart was always looking for you because I had

fallen in love with you. At first I didn't want to believe it could have happened like that—love at first sight—but when I kept missing you and wanting you so much, I had to admit to myself that it had."

"It is the same with me." She said the words against his neck.

"I love you, Angela," he said "So very much."

And his deep, passionate kiss confirmed what his words had told her. Travis loved her.

"In the next day or two I'm going to see an agent about a place I can rent for my business," Travis said after he had thoroughly kissed her again.

This news made her heart sing. They wouldn't be separated any more by all those kilometres.

"I don't need much space since I do just about every-thing on my computer," he told her.

"You could work from here," Angela suggested. "If you like." They hadn't spoken of living together and Angela thought perhaps she was assuming too much.

"Yes. Thank you for the kind invitation. But it's good to have a place just for work. Here, I'd be too distracted by your presence." He kissed the tip of her nose.

"I wouldn't be here very much," she said. "I spend most of my time at the shop. And at home I'm always looking for new things to introduce to my product line. Or designing new patterns. Or knitting. You could work in total peace."

"Seeing as I don't have a pad in Toronto and I don't really want to move in with Mom, how do you feel about us getting a place of our own?" Travis asked. "Something that's close to your shop and maybe even to my future place of work."

So he was thinking like she was—that being apart was not an option. "Yes, I would like that very much. Not being separated from you."

"And that reminds me," Travis said, getting up from the couch. "I brought something with me that I want to show you."

He dug in his suitcase and brought out a large, flat cardboard container, from which he pulled out a framed painting. Angela recognized it immediately. It was a painting based on the photo he had taken of her on the ship, after they had made love.

"Oh, it's beautiful!" she exclaimed. "You are a wonderful artist."

"Thank you. I like it very much. I brought it with me to show it to you and my mother. But now that I'm going to be living in Toronto, I'll just leave it with you till we have our own wall to hang it on." Travis held the painting at arm's length and looked at it critically. "It really does capture you, the way you looked after—"

Angela felt the heat rushing to her cheeks. "I know, I know," she quickly interrupted him. "But we can't have it out. It's too revealing."

Travis burst out in a booming laugh. "You're so modest! But you're right. I wouldn't want just anyone to be looking at you, the way your hair is in a tangle over your shoulders. And your lips . . . Ahh, those lips! We'll put it in our bedroom, where it will turn me on every night." He placed the painting on the couch against the backrest and reached for her. Brushing aside her hair, he murmured, "And every morning."

With a satisfied sigh Angela melted back into his arms.

"That is a beautiful painting!" Sylvia cried the minute she walked into the living room. "When did you get it?" With Jeff away bowling, she had come to spend the evening with Angela. The women were going to have dinner and have a good, old-fashioned chit-chat.

The painting of Angela still sat on the couch where Travis had left it. Sylvia picked it up and looked at it closely.

"Travis brought it with him from Calgary last night," Angela told her."He painted it."

"This is amazing. It's you, but what a sexy you it is! I have never seen you look like that." Sylvia laughed. "And for an obvious reason."

Oh, oh! Angela cringed. Now the questions would come flooding.

"You look absolutely luscious. Especially your lips. They look like someone has just kissed you deeply with great passion. Whew!"

"Oh, stop it, Sylvia," Angela tried to protest and wished she had taken the painting to the bedroom as had been her intention.

"I assume it's been painted from a photo. Do you have the original?"

"Yes, somewhere . . . I guess."

Sylvia held out a hand, palm up. "I'd like to compare. Or is that not allowed in the art world?"

"Only among very good friends," Angela said and went to get the photo from her bedroom where it was taped to the dresser mirror.

Sylvia peered at the picture closely and whistled. "It's beautiful. Where was it taken?"

Angela hesitated but then replied, "On the ship."

Sylvia turned to look at her and the "Oh-oh!" expression on her face told Angela that her game was up. True to her word, Sylvia hadn't mentioned Travis since their conversation in the spring, but Angela knew her friend had been dying a thousand deaths wanting to know the untold facts. Now the stories about no sparks between her and Travis would be exposed as not exactly so.

"With Travis? The 'No sparks at all guy'?"

"Yes, with Travis. And yes, there were sparks."

With that Angela proceeded to tell Sylvia everything—almost everything—that had happened between them on the boat. She told about Elaine and how shocked she had been about her death only three weeks before, and how she had refused to listen to Travis's explanations. And finally she told Sylvia what had ensued since he had reappeared in her life.

It felt good to have her best friend in her life again, sharing her good fortune.

"I think that is simply wonderful," Sylvia enthused. "I'm so happy for you. I'll get us some tea."

Angela laughed. "Tea is always the best way to celebrate, isn't it?"

"When we don't have champagne, yes," Sylvia said. "But celebrate we must, because it's about time someone special came into your life."

"My life was quite fine before Travis," Angela said defensively. "But now, however, it is much more than fine. It is wonderful," she added dreamily, causing Sylvia to burst out laughing.

"Oh, you dear lovebird! So now you're planning to move in together?" Sylvia poured the hot tea into cups. "That's another move for you after you've just settled in this nice condo."

"Yes, but I really don't mind," Angela said. "Moving in with Travis will be like moving to heaven," she cooed, hugging herself.

The preparations for the purchase of their condo were underway and Angela lived in a happy haze. She spent most of her spare time flipping through real estate pages and whenever a suite seemed like a possibility she and Travis went together to take a look at it. She wasn't even disappointed that Travis had refused her invitation to share her home for the time being and in the meanwhile he rented a room in his mother's house. He had found a small office for his landscaping design business not far from her shop and he often dropped by to eat his lunch with her.

"I know I'm being old-fashioned and maybe even kind of illogical," he tried to explain his reasoning as they sat in the tiny kitchen behind the shop, munching on sandwiches that Angela had made for him. "Especially since we're always having sex and all, but I want our together-home to be a first." He laughed, obviously embarrassed by his words. "Something special, maybe? I don't know how to explain it, but . . . that's how I feel."

Angela knew what he meant. Their together-home would be a symbol of starting a new life together.

He spent most of his evenings in her condo, and their love-making was as wonderful as ever. Each time they were in her bedroom, he looked at the painting of Angela on the wall and bragged that he'd done a fabulous job.

"But you, my darling, are much better in flesh," Travis always said as he reached for her. "I can't seem to get enough of you."

But why, then, hadn't he proposed to her? She found this bit disconcerting and wondered what he was waiting for. As far as she, herself, was concerned, she was ready to spend the rest of her life with him. Was he not as sure about his love for her?

But Angela tried to brush these feelings aside, even as she made preparations for their future. After all, these days many people lived together for years without being married. And some never did get married, but considered themselves as being in a forever relationship. Maybe that was how Travis saw things. And yet . . . he and Elaine *had* been married.

She mentioned this to Sylvia one evening when her friend once again dropped in for a cup of tea and a chat.

Sylvia laughed. "You're being much too anxious. I mean, how long have you two known each other?"

Angela wasn't convinced. "But is it really premature to expect him to be sure of his intentions? After all, we're buying a condo together."

"You know lots of people do that. As I told you, Jeff didn't proposed for three years. In fact I had to start dropping huge hints before he finally realized he should pop the question."

It was Angela's turn to laugh. "You're right. I guess men don't see things quite the same way women do." She set cups and a plate of cookies on the coffee table in the living room and poured the tea. "Have some cookies. Marita made them and gave me a dozen. They are delicious. She is such a fabulous cook, my brother will soon turn into a chubby but happy hubby."

Sylvia sipped her tea and bit into a cookie, not even reacting to Angela's funny quip. Angela felt that something seemed to be bothering her friend, for she looked slightly preoccupied.

"Is something the matter?" Angela at last asked.

"No, not really. It's just that I took the subway downtown yesterday to look for winter jackets that were on sale," Sylvia began. Then she took another bite of her cookie. "These are really good."

"Yes, they are." What was Sylvia driving at?

After more hesitation, Sylvia opened up. "Guess what I saw on an ad in the train?"

"I give up. What did you see?"

"I saw a lipstick ad and I swear it had the exact same face that's in the painting Travis made of you. Of course it had a wide-brimmed black hat covering most of the face, but the nose and lips are—"

Angela burst out laughing. "You are kidding! That is impossible."

"Maybe it is, but it sure looked the same. Would you mind if I took a peek at the painting?"

"Sure." Angela got up and went into the bedroom with Sylvia.

Sylvia scrutinized the painting. Then she walked over and covered part of the forehead and eyes with her hand. "Sure looks the same," she said. "But of course, as you said, it's not possible."

They returned to the living room and Angela dismissed Sylvia's words by picking up a pattern book. She flipped to a page and showed it to Sylvia. "I like this vest pattern. What do you think? Should I knit it for the shop?"

Sylvia only glanced at the design and ignored Angela's question. "You could still see the woman's closed eyelids, her nose and the lips. Especially the lips. They sure looked like yours in the painting. They were luscious."

Angela waved her hand. "But they were not mine." This topic was done. "I think I'll start this vest tonight. It won't take too long, and I need more ready-made items for the shop."

"But if you're ever riding on the subway, remember to take a look," Sylvia persisted.

"I promise," Angela said and got up. "I will make the vest a nice forest green with sunny yellow flecks here and there. I have just the right wool for it right here at home."

Angela put up the "Closed" sign and ran out of the shop and across the street to pick up a coffee. The morning had been slow and she had already finished the pot she had made for herself at lunch time. Since the afternoon was almost over she didn't feel like brewing another pot, and had decided to run across the street for a cup. That was all she needed to perk herself up.

As she stood waiting to order a take-out in the busy little restaurant, she picked up a magazine from a pile that was on the counter. She flipped through a few pages and then stopped. Good grief! There was the ad Sylvia had been telling her about! It was a whole page ad of a woman's head with the brim of a black hat covering the forehead, but show-ing the eyelids, nose and the lips. It was definitely her own face!

This was unreal! Her hands shook as she contin-ued to stare at the picture, until she became aware that the waitress behind the counter was patiently waiting for her to order. At last the managed to cough out, "Large coffee, please. Black."

She kept staring at the picture while the waitress held out the take-out cup to her.

"Miss? Here's your coffee," the girl at last said.

"Oh, sorry. Thank you." Angela dug the money out of her purse with unsteady hands. "I'll take this magazine, too."

Back at the store she opened up the magazine with hands that still shook. The face certainly looked like the one in Travis' painting, but of course that couldn't be. It was impossible. Besides, most of the face was covered by the black brim of the hat, so maybe it wasn't her.

But it was. She couldn't wait to get home and compare the ad with the painting. She hoped it was simply an uncanny similarity and she could laugh about it to Sylvia tonight.

As she drove home after work, she felt so distracted she was afraid she would cause an accident. There she marched directly into the bedroom and began to compare the ad with the painting. She frowned in disbelief. They were identical. She looked again more closely, peering in turn at the painting and at the magazine ad. There was no question in her mind about it. Except for the black hat, the two were absolutely identical, right down to the smallest detail.

Dismayed, she turned away from the painting, crushed the magazine in her hands and flung it aside. How could Travis have done this? How could he have sold the painting to a cosmetic firm? On the ship he had told her the photo of her was his most treasured memory. And he had said the painting would be hung in their bedroom so no other eyes would see it.

Angela snorted. Sure, no other eyes except half the city's since—as Sylvia had told her—it was also in the subway cars. She walked up to the painting and lifted it off the wall. She simply couldn't look at it any longer. A huge tear dropped from her eye onto the canvas as she pushed the painting under the bed.

In the living room she flopped onto the couch and tried to think about this logically. Perhaps Travis had sold the painting because he was short of money? Surely not. But what other explanation was there for this? Nothing she tried to think of made any sense.

Was everything she had learned about him since he'd come back into her life again only a lie? A deception? Was he really the cold-hearted, callous man who would have sex with the first available woman after his wife's death? A man who would sell something precious—or something he had vowed was precious—when offered a good deal?

She hugged herself as shivers racked her body.

Chapter Ten

Travis unlocked the mailbox in the foyer of his mother's apartment building and pulled out a bunch of ads. A long business envelope addresses to him was the only item of importance there today. In his room he sliced it open and was astounded to find a sizeable cheque from John's advertising company. The accompanying letter told him it was for his contribution to the lipstick ad John had created for "Beauty Plus".

With a puzzled frown, Travis immediately dialed John's number.

"What the hell is going on?" he began without any preliminaries. "What's with this lipstick ad for 'Beauty Plus'? And why did you send me this huge cheque? What do I have to do with 'Beauty Plus'? Or with any lipstick ad for that matter?"

He heard John's laughter at the other end of the line. "Didn't you see the ad I enclosed?"

Travis looked again in the envelope and pulled out a folded paper. When he opened it, his jaw dropped. It was a picture of a woman wearing a black hat with a brim. And the face was unmistakably the face of Angela!

John's laughter irritated him. "This is Angela's face," he said.

"Yeah that's right," John agreed, still sounding very pleased with himself.

Travis frowned. "How on earth did you get Angela to agree to pose for it?"

"I didn't. I created the ad from the painting. Isn't it fabulous?" Now John's voice sounded triumphant.

"What painting?" Travis asked, although he already suspected he knew the answer.

"Remember when I visited you when you were working on the painting of the dark-haired beauty?"

"The painting of Angela. I remember." So that was it! Travis stiffened with anger while John warbled on with no idea that his friend was ready to explode.

"Remember how I took a photo of the painting? Everyone thinks the lips are exquisitely lovely the way they—"

"You made an ad from my painting?" Travis asked, his voice seething with fury. "Without asking me?"

"I did." John sounded proud rather than apolo-getic. Either he didn't hear the anger in Travis's voice or he chose to ignore it. "And it was an overnight success, believe me. I know if I had asked you, you would have refused, being the kind of guy you are. But have you taken a look at the cheque? I gave you a third of what they paid me!" John sounded extremely pleased with his generosity.

If John had been here in the room he would have been lying flat on the floor by now. "The reason I would have refused is not because I'm 'that kind of a guy' as you put it," Travis spoke through gritted teeth. "I would have refused because this woman means everything to me and this painting is something very special between us."

There was silence at the other end. Then John, finally sounding contrite, quietly said, "Geesh, I'm sorry, Travis, I thought you'd be pleased the ad is such a success. And I thought you'd be happy with the surprise cheque I sent you. Kind of like an early Christmas present."

Travis sighed and for a few moments he didn't reply. He knew if he said anything now it would not be polite. "John, you are an absolute, incredible ass," he at last pronounced. "I'm afraid this thing will blow up right in my face."

"What do you mean?" John asked. Contrition was now all over the words.

"If only you had asked me first. I can only imagine

Angela's reaction if she's seen this ad . . ."

"I'm sorry, Travis," John apologized again. Then he brightened up. "But maybe she *likes* the ad. Have you thought about that? Most people would be proud to have pictures of themselves plastered all over the subway cars."

"Subway cars? John, I think I better hang up before I . . . before I . . ." With that Travis disconnected and slumped into an armchair. He could only hope Angela wouldn't see the ad before he had a chance to explain the circumstances. Maybe, just maybe, a catastrophe could be averted.

He desperately wanted to avoid what had happened in his cabin during the cruise She had walked out and refused to listen to his side of the story. If she saw the ad he knew what her reaction would be. And rightfully so. She would think he was some greedy cad out to make a quick buck by selling something that he had told her was precious to him.

She would think he had sold her out. What other explanation could she give to herself when she saw her face on all the subway cars? Her lovely face that exposed her feelings after their stormy love-making. Her lips, glowing and full after his fervent kisses, her hair disheveled, her eyes brilliant and dewy with the after-glow of passionate sex. It was a portrait of love—of their private love—that now was out for all the world to see. She would be totally crushed if—when—she saw it. There was no way he could prevent her from seeing it.

His hands were far from steady as he dialed her number.

But there was no answer.

Angela opened her door and Sylvia entered, immediately enfolding her in a warm hug.

"Thanks you for coming over on such a short notice, Sylvia."

"Hey, any time, my dear," Sylvia said. "You sounded like you really needed some comforting. Jeff was worried and thought maybe he should come, too, but I figured maybe you would prefer girl talk."

Angela dabbed her eyes. The sight of her old friend already made her feel slightly better. "You are right. Though that was nice of Jeff to want to help."

They went into the living room and Sylvia placed a bottle of red wine on the coffee table before seating herself on the sofa. "I also thought a bit of wine might help. Bring out a couple of glasses, will you?"

Angela set down two wine goblets. "Thank you. Though you really didn't have to, because I do have a few bottles in the cupboard."

Sylvia unscrewed the cap and poured out the red wine. She raised her glass. "Here's to getting rid of whatever is bugging you."

Angela sat down with a deep sigh. It was difficult to start talking and admit to Sylvia what an idiot she had been. For the last two days she had refused to talk to Travis, though he had called repeatedly. There was no way he could justify his actions. It was almost sacrilegious what he had done, allowing the so-called precious photo to be made into an ad for lipstick. That was simply shameful and as far as she was concerned, was a non-redeemable act.

Tonight she had sat at the kitchen table for a long time, crying her eyes out, before picking up the phone and calling Sylvia. She wanted to hear it from her best friend how stupid she was where men were concerned. It didn't seem to be enough to just keep repeating it to herself and calling herself all manner of names.

She swallowed."I'm such an idiot, Sylvia."

"How exactly?"

Angela took a deep breath and slowly began. "I have always been proud of being perceptive as far as people are concerned." She swallowed again. "I always thought I could read people and tell just by looking into their eyes when they were being honest and when they were being deceitful."

"That would be a good skill," Sylvia put in but left it at that.

"Yes, it would, if I had it. But I have now seen that I don't have it at all." She grabbed a tissue from the coffee table and blew her nose. This was more difficult than she had imagined, but she felt she had to go through this ordeal and get it all out in the open and, hopefully, out of her system.

"Remember how I thought Steve was such a good friend. I thought he was being honest with me when he said he was divorced and had no children."

"Yes, I remember."

"And it turned out he had two cute little daughters and a poor wife who knew nothing about her husband's lies. Or at least I assume she knew nothing."

"That's their problem, not yours," Sylvia put in wisely.

"That's true. And I don't really care anything about his marital situation. Except that his two daughters are so cute that I feel bad for them."

"Okay. But they aren't your problem, either."

"You are right, Sylvia. My problem is that I thought Steve was a friend. I thought I could see in his eyes that he was a good man." Angela held her tissue, ready to dab her eyes should they start to fill. "He was a louse. And I could not tell."

"Maybe he was such a smart louse that he could look a person in the eye like he's a totally honest Joe. There are such people."

"Yes." Angela took a gulp of her wine. "Or then I'm just not able to tell the difference."

Sylvia refilled both glasses. "Listen, there are such professional cads that no one can tell the difference. Please don't blame yourself."

But here was Travis, also, who had deceived her. Could it really be that she had met two professional cads one after the other? "No," she said, shaking her head. "I just couldn't tell. And here I was just so sure I could." She sipped her wine. "I am just an idiot."

"I hate to disagree, but I disagree," Sylvia said, pointing at Angela with her wine glass. "This one situation does not make you an idiot."

"Yes, if it were just this one situation!" Angela cried earnestly. "But it is not! There is also . . . " She swallowed. "There is also Travis," she finished quietly.

"Okay." Sylvia took a large gulp of her wine. "So I assume this has to do with the painting and the ads on the subway?"

"Yes. But even more than that. I told you he was already deceitful on the ship. He is much worse than Steve." She took another sip.

"But you told me he explained all that," Sylvia said calmly.

"I thought he had explained it all to me and we had settled it all, but after this . . . I don't think he has been telling me the truth about *anything*." For a few moments she was unable to continue, and Sylvia waited silently beside her. After blowing her nose again, Angela continued, while Sylvia refilled their glasses.

"On the ship, just after we had . . . " she left unsaid what had happened. It was too painful. But she knew Sylvia understood. "He told me his wife had died just three weeks before he came on the cruise. I was devastated. We had had such a great time together, and I couldn't believe he could be so unfeeling as to have an affair just weeks after his wife was gone."

Sylvia shook her head. "Yes, that does seem unbelievable," she said.

"But after we met again he explained it all, and I believed him when he told me he had been faithful to her all those years when she was ill."

"So that makes him a good guy, doesn't it?" Sylvia put in sounding hopeful.

"Yes. I thought so. But what about the ad in all the subway cars and magazines? How can that be explained away?"

"I don't know," Sylvia mused. "It really does put him in a nasty light, doesn't it?"

"Yes. He is just a deceitful cad," Angela exclaimed. It seemed that all the pieces were falling into place now and she could think much more clearly. "I think the story about his wife's illness was just a bunch of lies, too."

"You are probably right," Sylvia said and poured the last of the wine into her glass. She held up the empty bottle. "Did you say you had some wine stashed away somewhere?"

Angela went to fetch another bottle and unscrewed the cap. "Travis is just like Jason in high school. Remember him?"

"I sure do!" Sylvia exclaimed vehemently. "You couldn't believe a single word that fellow ever said." She raised her glass. "Here's to Jason, the biggest liar of Muirhead High!"

Angela took a hefty gulp from her glass. Then she giggled. "He sure could spin a fabulous tale. Remember when he told everyone that he had a pet monkey? He made that fictional animal sound so real that I totally believed him."

Sylvia hooted. "So did I! I even begged him if I could come over to his house and visit, so I could pet a real live monkey."

Angela laughed so hard she almost spilled her wine. "I'll bet all he had was a stuffed Gorgeous George! He probably took it to bed with him every night!"

Sylvia's face became serious. "I wonder if he was lonely. Maybe that's why he told everyone about a real monkey. Maybe he was just an unhappy boy who hugged his toy against him at night to give him comfort."

Angela dabbed her eyes that were filling with tears. "Poor Jason! To think we were so mean to him. We all teased him when we found out he didn't have a real monkey after all. Oh, I feel so awful!" She blew her nose again. "I wonder if I'm getting a cold. I keep having to blow my nose all the time."

"It's sadness that makes a person's nose run," Sylvia explained and took another sip of wine. "That's why you were blowing your nose all the time you told me about Travis."

"Travis!" Angela wailed. "Oh, that is so terrible. But he is not Jason with a pet monkey. He's a man with a dead wife."

"But he did have a monkey at Gibraltar, didn't he?" Sylvia asked.

Angela burst into gales of laughter. "Yes, you are so right! That was *his* fake monkey."

"Except it was a real monkey," Sylvia pointed out.

"Yes, but it wasn't *his* monkey. He didn't own it. Just like Jason didn't own a monkey. So they are both liars." It didn't quite make as much sense as she first thought it might, but it sounded reasonable enough for Sylvia to nod in agreement.

"Except Jason had a stuffed monkey. Travis doesn't,"

Angela mused. "So which one of them is the worse liar?"

"But we don't know if Jason had a stuffed monkey," Sylvia pointed out.

Angela frowned. "I thought you said he had a Gorgeous George monkey."

Sylvia shook her head vigorously. "No, *you* said he had one. *I* didn't say anything."

"Well, did he or didn't he?" This puzzle was beginning to annoy her.

"I don't know. I don't think we'll ever know."

Angela dabbed her eyes. "Poor Jason."

At that moment the phone rang on the table in front of her. She picked it up and froze when she heard Travis's voice.

"Angela," he said. "We have to talk."

Angela held the phone away from her and looked at Sylvia who shook her head.

"I'm sorry, Travis, but you and Jason both lied about the monkeys. I do not want to speak to you." And then, for emphasis she added. "Ever."

There was a silence at the other end and then in a hesitating voice Travis asked, "Uh . . . What monkeys? Who is Jason?"

"I am sorry, Jason, but I am not going to speak to you about it. Ever." And with that she hung up.

When she looked triumphantly at Sylvia for approval, she found to her dismay that her friend's head had fallen to her breast and she had dozed off.

Angela shrugged and proceeded to dial Jeff's number.

The next morning was Sunday. Angela woke with a tremendous hangover and, holding her aching head, she shuffled to the kitchen to make herself some herbal tea. Not having ever suffered from a hangover, she had no idea whether herbal tea would help her feel better, but she figured it couldn't hurt.

Just as she had settled down on a kitchen chair to sip the hot beverage, the buzzer sounded, announcing a visitor.

Without answering, she pressed the button to let the person in and soon was face to face with Travis.

"Angela, what the hell is going on with you?" he burst out the moment he stepped in. "Last night you didn't make any sense at all. Calling me Jason. And talking about monkeys. What was going on here?"

"Sylvia was visiting and we were talking," Angela said without elaborating further.

But that seemed to be enough for Travis to get an inkling of what had possibly happened. "You two were drinking."

Angela grimaced. "Yes."

"Who is Jason?" His voice now held a smile and sounded very gentle, as though he knew what Angela was going though at this moment. This made her feel even more terrible. He sounded just the way he had on the ship—gentle and kind.

"He is a boy we knew in high school," she replied and took a sip of her tea. "But Travis, I do not want to speak to you. Please leave."

"But Angela, please let me explain," he implored, holding out his hands. "I understand you think I have let you down. And I'm not here to make excuses, but I want you to know that—"

But Angela didn't want to hear his explanations. Her head throbbed and she felt horrible. "No," she snapped. "I want you to go. Please leave."

Travis' eyes shot open in surprise, and immediately Angela was ashamed of her outburst. But it had the desired effect. Travis left and Angela reached for a tissue to blow her nose.

Angela was waiting on a customer at the boutique when the phone rang. She excused herself and went to answer and was surprised to hear Mrs. Jordan's voice. For a moment she was too shocked to speak. "May I call you back?" she at last stammered. "I have a customer."

When the woman had left, Angela hesitated for a few minutes before dialing Mrs. Jordan's number.

"Thank you so much for calling me back," Travis'

mother said. She sounded just as kind and gentle as she had at her birthday party, and Angela couldn't help warming up to her.

"I don't want to hold you up," Mrs. Jordan continued. "I just wanted to invite you for tea this Sunday afternoon. If you recall, that was something we talked about at my party, and I thought it's about time we finally did it. Would Sunday be convenient for you?"

"Yes, Sunday will be fine," Angela admitted, although she had been hoping that her dealings with the Jordans were now over. But there was no way she could refuse the kind invitation. And it was true, they had already been talking about it at the party.

So on Sunday afternoon she drove to Mrs. Jordan's home with a fluttering heart, desperately hoping that Travis wouldn't also be there. She was afraid he might be behind the invitation and was using it as an excuse to talk to her. She hadn't asked, of course, but was hoping that the tea invitation was just for the mother and herself.

Mrs. Jordan let her in and Angela sighed with relief when she entered the living room and found that Travis was not sitting there.

After some chatting about the weather and how things were going at Angela's boutique, Mrs. Jordan brought out the tea tray.

Angela reached for a wafer while balancing her teacup on her lap. "This is so lovely," she commented. "Makes me think of a British movie. It's so un-like anything one might see when visiting a Spanish home."

"Yes, I can imagine it would be quite different," Mrs. Jordan said and then, rather abruptly, came to the point. "I want to thank you for coming, Angela," she said. "I wanted to tell you how happy I am that Travis has at last found a wonderful person to share his life with. He is so very fond of you."

Angela felt a blush rise to her cheeks. So the lady had no idea of the fact that she and Travis were no longer a couple. "We haven't really talked about those things," she said, feeling like a deceitful liar.

"Oh, I apologize if my words made you uncomfortable. I didn't mean to embarrass you. Of course I'm speaking strictly from Travis's side of the fence. But it's been so very long since I've seen my son this happy."

"I'm glad he's happy, because he has told me something of his past, and it sounds very sad." Angela was afraid if they continued speaking about her and Travis, the recent events between them might somehow slip into the conversation. But she couldn't prevent Mrs. Jordan from talking since the invitation had obviously been extended for a reason.

And the reason soon became clear. It was obvious

Mrs. Jordan wanted to tell her about Travis's past. "Yes. It was very sad," the lady said with a sigh. "Elaine was a wonderful woman and they were very much in love."

"Yes, I gathered that. It is wonderful that they loved each other." Where was Mrs. Jordan going with this?

"Many people with MS can live almost a normal life span. Unfortunately Elaine's case was the worst possible scenario."

"Yes. Travis explained that to me." Angela herself had also done some research on it, so she knew about the disease.

"We tried to remain positive, but she went down so very quickly." Mrs. Jordan bit into her forgotten biscuit and took a sip of her tea. "Travis remained a faithful husband even when there was no real marriage between them. Right to the end."

"Yes. He told me," Angela whispered.

"I'm glad you understand. He is a good man. A very good man."

"Yes." Angela had to force out the words and gulped some tea to wet her throat. Obviously Mrs. Jordan knew nothing of the ad on the subway trains and magazines. Was she trying to defend Travis and his actions on the cruise? Angela doubted Mrs. Jordan knew the details, but perhaps she was trying to tell Angela that even though Elaine had died only weeks before the cruise, Travis had not behaved improperly, no matter what had happened between him and Angela. Of course it was all speculation on the lady's part, but at her age Mrs. Jordan could probably make a pretty educated guess.

"When Travis came home from the cruise, he was so down," Mrs. Jordan went on. "At first I thought it was because he missed Elaine, but then he told me on the phone that he had met a lovely woman on the cruise but nothing had come of it. I knew he really missed you."

"Yes. We didn't meet for almost a year," Angela said. "It was quite serendipitous that Travis happened to walk into my store to look for a gift for you." She returned Mrs. Jordan's smile, and hoped it didn't look too forced.

"What I really wanted to say to you, my dear, is that just because a person has loved someone very much, there is no reason that this person can't love again, just as deeply."

"Is that why you asked me to come today?"

"Yes. I am hoping that one of these days—"

"I think he is a very fine man," Angela said, cutting Mrs. Jordan off. She didn't want to hear about what the lady wished for the future, because that was never going to happen.

Mrs. Jordan put her teacup on the table. "I am so

very happy for you both. I know you have been looking for a condo and I do hope you find a nice one soon so you can settle down together."

Angela wanted to cry. That was what she, herself, had been hoping for with all her heart, but now . . . She frowned in confusion. Was it possible that Travis was not the deceitful, cold and unfeeling man that in her mind she had painted him to be? His mother seemed to think that the sun rose and set on him. Could Angela be wrong? Maybe she should have listened to his explanation when he came to see her the previous week. He had told her he knew she felt he had let her down, but he had wanted to explain.

And again, like the time on the ship, she had refused to give him that chance.

Travis dialed Angela's number. He *had* to try again! He couldn't just give up without trying to explain to her what had happened. At least he could then feel he had tried to vindicate himself. Maybe she would refuse to accept his explanation, but at least he would have tried.

This time, to his surprise and relief, after several rings she answered.

"Could I come to pick you up from the store and take you to dinner tonight?" he asked and waited with trepidation for her reply. He fully expected it to be negative, and was armed with more persuasive tactics.

"Yes. That would be fine," she said and almost caused him to keel over in surprise.

Travis was puzzled. She sounded very sedate and not the least bit angry. For the life of him he couldn't tell what message her tone of voice conveyed. He would have to wait till six o'clock to find out.

Right when Angela was putting up the "Closed" sign Travis parked his car at the curb. She came out, locked the door of the boutique and then walked to the car. He was standing on the sidewalk, ready to open the door for her, but she didn't look at him. She simply got into his car and buckled herself in without a word.

"I'm glad you came, Angela," he said, though he was still totally in the woods as to her reason for accepting his invitation.

He pulled off the curb and drove for a couple of blocks before she turned to him and spoke.

"Where are we going for dinner?"

Travis was confused. Did she just pretend to sound cheerful? And was that a genuine smile?

"I thought we would go somewhere special tonight," he replied and waited for her reaction.

"Oh? Why somewhere special?"

For the life of him Travis couldn't figure her out.

She actually sounded sociable. Did he dare think friendly? Where was the negativity of the past weeks?

Before John had dropped the bombshell, he had been planning a special evening when he would take her out for dinner at a ritzy place and ask her to marry him. But now he didn't know if tomorrow he would be returning the ring back to the store. He had to try. Nothing ventured, nothing gained.

"Because I'm happy you agreed to come," he said, answering her question.

It being the dinner hour, the downtown restaurant he had chosen was full, but the hum of conversation was not overpowering. He had managed to book a table after he had called her, and they now followed the hostess to their places.

Travis ordered the wine and after they had chosen their meals, they sat and observed the other customers around them. Travis didn't know whether he should wait till after they had eaten, or find out now what the situation with the advertisement was. Without thinking any more about it, he made his decision and blurted out, "Have you ridden on the subway lately?"

Angela looked up, her dark eyes big with surprise. "Why do you ask?" she said and then sipped her wine.

Something about her looked too phony. Travis was

sure she had seen the ad and was just playing him like a fish on a hook. Enough of this.

"Because you think I'm a horrible, greedy cad who sold the portrait to an advertising company," he pronounced firmly, letting her know he saw through her act. "And I can't blame you." He took a gulp of wine to fortify himself but it didn't seem to help. His stomach was still in a knot, waiting for her reaction.

"There *is* an explanation," he said. But probably she wouldn't think much of it.

"Is there?"

"Yes. And I have told John to remove every last one of those ads everywhere in the transit system."

"Who is John?" Angela asked.

Travis grimaced. He obviously wasn't going about this very logically. Now that he had his moment to explain, he was too nervous and was blowing it. "John is a friend of mine," he said. "I should say he *was* a friend of mine."

"Tell me about it," she said.

Wha-at? She was asking for clarification! This was not like the time on the ship when she had walked out on him and had refused to listen to his side of the situation.

"I've known John for years," Travis began, trying to make his explanation logical. "He's just starting out with his advertising business. I know John thought he was doing me a big favour by using the painting for the lipstick ad, but he didn't know how precious that photo was to me. I let him see it because he was a good friend. A trusted friend. But I have told him he must have them all taken down. I don't care if it costs him his client. He shouldn't have done it behind my back." He looked at her earnestly. "So you see, I didn't sell you out. Though I can understand when you saw your face on all the subway cars, you thought I had. Your lovely face—the portrait of my love for you—and there it was for all the world to see! You must have been totally crushed when you saw it. And I was, too. Crushed and desperate, because I couldn't prevent you from seeing it."

She looked at him over the rim of her wine glass. "I actually did not see it on the subway or a bus. I saw it in a magazine."

Travis felt his heart drop down to his stomach and the wine he had just sipped went down the wrong way. "Oh God!" he gasped between coughs. "They're in magazines, too?"

"Yes, it seems they are," she said.

After he had finished his coughing fit, he looked directly at Angela and shook his head. "I am so very sorry. I don't think I can do anything about that."

"No, I guess you can't." Her level, almost unemotional tone made him want to get up and leave in defeat. He was toast.

Then she cocked her head to one side, making her look like she wasn't angry. "But I think you have done your best."

Travis's heart leapt back up to his chest and beat there, full of hope. But he wanted her to understand exactly how he felt about this mess. "Angela, I can't blame you for being angry, because I'm furious. And the cheque my friend—my *former* friend—sent, is in the garbage. I ripped it up."

He reached over to grasp her hand and was relieved when she didn't pull hers away. "Angela, I love you so much. Please forgive me for having been so careless with the photo and the painting."

"You trusted your friend. That was only natural," Angela said, and Travis finally believed that she was not condemning him to the purgatory for the rest of his life.

"And it doesn't sound like your friend meant to do any harm," she went on, slowly raising him to Seventh Heaven. "As you said, he probably thought he was doing you a favour."

"Darling," he muttered and gripped both her hands in his.

"I'm sorry it happened," Angela continued. "But what I am really sorry about is that I refused to listen to you when you tried to explain it. I almost committed the same mistake again that I did on the ship."

"You had every reason to get angry," Travis put in, but she silenced him with a shake of her head.

"Nevertheless, I should have been more open to hearing you out. To acknowledge that there *could* be an explanation for all this. It makes me shudder to think that because of this, we could have been separated forever."

"No, we wouldn't have, because I would never have given you up," Travis vehemently stated. "I would have pursued you to the ends of the earth till you listened to me."

Angela smiled at his forceful words and the sight of her face again glowing with happiness proved once and for all that she had accepted his explanation.

"I guess trust is the underlying factor here," she mused. "You trusted your friend when perhaps you shouldn't have. And I didn't trust you, when I should have. In my heart I knew you weren't a mercenary type who would sell the portrait. Everything I had found out about you since you came back to my life—everything your family told me, everything you said and did—told me you were a fine human being. I should have trusted that something else had happened regarding the portrait, and it wasn't that you had sold it. Now I know what it was."

Travis felt in his pocket for the little box that he

had carried with him for weeks, hoping against hope that eventually this thing would sort itself out. Now, at last, was the moment he had been waiting for. In the crowded restaurant he got up, dug the ring box out of his pocket and went around to Angela's side of the table. There he dropped down on one knee beside her.

"Angela, I love you with all my heart," he said looking up at her. "Will you please marry me?"

She gave a little cry of surprise and covered her mouth in delight. "Oh, Travis, darling, of course I'll marry you."

She opened the box and took out the sparkling diamond ring, which Travis then slipped on her finger. He stood up and pulled her into his arms.

"They've seen your lovely face all over the city," he murmured. "So now they can see why it looked the way it did in that painting." And as he kissed her deeply, the couples at the nearby tables clapped and cheered in delight.

Epilogue

In the Cordova solarium Travis stood at the make-
shift altar with his brother and the clergyman by his
side, waiting for the bridal procession to enter. The
sun shone through the windowpanes while outside
the snow banks glittered with a million diamonds
and Mrs. Cordova's beloved plants bloomed with
bright, colourful flowers, although it was already late
November.

Music was provided by the childish voice of Aleksi
Laine, the little son of Mika and Anna-Liisa. The family had flown from Finland for the ceremony and now
Aleksi was belting out a lovely Finnish song to enter-
tain the guests. It was unfortunate that no one but
Anna-Liisa and her two other children, Elise and Johannes, could understand the words, but Travis
could see Anna-Liisa dabbing her eyes, indicating that
the message was obviously meaningful.

Shaylee and Michael stood with their baby daughter,

Aurora, in his arms, and Marita kept André and Alexander under control while Miguel was involved with his duties.

Soon the doors of the solarium opened and one of Travis's little nieces, dressed in a pale pink fluffy dress, came in, scattering rose petals from her basket as she approached the altar. She was followed by Sylvia, wearing a close-fitting dark blue satin dress and carrying a small bouquet of dark red roses. As she passed by, she smiled broadly at all the wedding guests on both sides of the carpeted aisle.

And finally in walked Angela in a long white gown on Miguel's arm. Travis's heart gave a leap when he saw that her long, dark hair was flowing free onto her shoulders, adorned only by a small, white flower.

After the short ceremony everyone came to congratulate the new couple. Shaylee and Michael kissed them on both cheeks, while Mika and Anna-Liisa enfolded both Travis and Angela in warm hugs.

"I'm so happy I could cry!" Travis' mother kept repeating and wiped away tears that kept flowing, although she, herself, was smiling from ear to ear.

Marita now unleashed the twins and allowed them to run and grab the legs of their father and Auntie Angela. Miguel hoisted them up into the air and they added to the pandemonium with their shrieks.

Elise, Anna-Liisa's daughter, came up and shyly

gave Angela a painting she had done. "It's a picture of a scene in Finland," she explained. "I did it and Mika thought it was good enough to give as a wedding gift. I hope you like it."

Johannes, Elise's brother, then handed Travis a wood carving of a reindeer. "We have those in Lapland," he said by way of explanation.

While everyone was enjoying the delicious meal that Marita had organized and mostly prepared herself, Travis pulled Angela into a corner of the room and wrapped his arms around her.

"Hello, Mrs. Jordan," he whispered. "I am so happy you chose me for your husband."

"I had no choice," Angela whispered back. "I had to marry the father of my child."

Travis frowned, puzzled. "What do you mean?" he asked.

Angela smiled mischievously. "That little careless misstep of ours late last summer has had unexpected results. Or perhaps I should say expected ones?"

Travis's eyes flew open and his jaw dropped. "Darling, you're not . . .?"

"Yes, I am. So get prepared for fatherhood, Mr. Jordan."

Travis slapped his forehead and laughed with joy. "That is the best wedding present you could have given me!" he exclaimed.

"That is good, because I had nothing else in mind to give you."

"Except yourself," Travis said, nuzzling her neck. "And that is all I ever wanted."

About Karen Rossi

Karen Rossi (the pen name of Kaarina Brooks) has been a romantic since she was a child. She and her sister had their own "publishing company" and wrote about love-struck princes and princesses.

Today she writes grown-up romances where modern-day "princes and princesses" go through heart-wrenching relationship struggles before reaching their happily ever after.

She now also has a real publishing company, Wisteria Publications. Besides romances, she also publishes kids' books and non-fiction works, such as a cook book.

She lives in Southern Ontario with her husband and kitty-cat, Lilly.

www.wisteriapublications.com
brooks.kaarina@gmail.com